All [illegible] Alaskan [illegible]tains . . .

There was the chance the Russian team would slip past his hiding spot, missing him completely. If so, the colonel might strike the battle's initial blow as he'd wanted to all along. The trick would be to remain absolutely still, praying the man on point would be so absorbed in yesterday's trail that he would miss whatever sign Chuikov had left while backtracking. If the commandos bypassed him, he could drop back onto *their* trail and possibly take at least one man out of the equation facing him. For fifteen minutes the Russian willed himself to become part of the stone surrounding him. There were no sounds from the narrow opening behind him, and the returning sounds of the forest assured him his hunters were now well past his lair.

Now Chuikov would become the hunter . . .

Books in the SPRINGBLADE series by Greg Walker

SPRINGBLADE
MACHETE
STILETTO
BOWIE

BORDER MASSACRE
(coming in October)

BOWIE

GREG WALKER

C

CHARTER BOOKS, NEW YORK

BOWIE

A Charter Book/published by arrangement with
the author

PRINTING HISTORY
Charter edition/July 1990

ISBN: 1-55773-353-8

Charter Books are published by The Berkley Publishing Group,
200 Madison Avenue, New York, New York 10016.
The name "CHARTER" and the "C" logo
are trademarks belonging to Charter Communications, Inc.

PRINTED IN THE UNITED STATES OF AMERICA

10 9 8 7 6 5 4 3 2 1

BOWIE is dedicated to Gene Scroft and the twenty-four other journalists who were killed in 1989 while covering wars in far-off, mostly forgotten countries like Peru, Burma, India, Mozambique, Sri Lanka, the Philippines, Cambodia, and Burundi. While Americans fret about what's happening in the lives of the rich and famous, a select group of writers and correspondents are trekking across the jungles, deserts, and mountains of countries we would never otherwise hear about except through their efforts. They are soldiers in their own right, and they have died as such far too often.

Greg Walker
September 89

BOWIE

CHAPTER 1

Checking the rearview mirror of his rented Grand Am, Colonel Peter Chuikov assured himself he wasn't being followed, at least not yet. Flipping the turn signal on, he slipped his rented sedan over one lane, deftly wheeling the nondescript automobile into the mall parking lot. He spotted a bank of pay phones conveniently located near the main entrance.

Parking the car, Chuikov lifted a Beretta 92-F off the seat next to him and slipped it behind his back. The big automatic held fifteen rounds in its magazine, plus a sixteenth in the tube. The Spetsnaz officer had purchased the weapon from a small gun store soon after landing in Valdez, snapping up two extra magazines as well as an extra hundred rounds of CCI hollow-points. Chuikov preferred the Beretta to other 9-mm auto loaders, primarily because it could function under the worst of conditions. He'd carried one during his year in Afghanistan, where conditions had been indeed grim. He'd been delighted to find the 92 available, paying for it in cash and using one of the KGB's excellent forged Alaskan driver's licenses as proof of his residency.

The weapon secured in his waistband, Chuikov stepped from the car and hurried toward an open booth on the end. There were few people about, the hour still early for shoppers. He returned the smile of an attractive blond who had just finished a call of her own, checking her out as she walked past. In reality he was covering his own ass, knowing that as unlikely as it might seem, Suworov might have discovered his defection already and have activated his network of agents in the Anchorage area.

The blond glanced back at the handsome man with the ash-colored hair, deciding to throw a little more action into her hips as she walked. His approving smile pleased her, and for a moment she thought of several excuses to return to the phone she'd just left. A glance at her watch told her she was already nearly late for work, and with a sigh she hurried up the sidewalk, aware of the man's eyes on her with every provocative step she took.

Chuikov watched the young woman disappear into the mall. Satisfied she wouldn't pop back out with a pistol in her hand, he grabbed the black receiver from its cradle and fed a series of numbers into the phone's computerized memory. Within seconds the connection was made. Chuikov leaned back against the cool glass of the booth so he could watch everything around him while waiting for someone to answer at the other end.

"Special Operations Command, Staff Sergeant Ivanov speaking. May I help you, sir?" The noncom's Russian name startled Chuikov for a moment, but he quickly recovered, asking if Colonel Tom Foster was in. "The colonel just arrived, sir. Can I tell him who's calling?"

"Certainly, Sergeant. Tell Colonel Foster that Peter Chuikov would like a moment of his time. He knows who I am."

Several seconds went by as the sergeant kept him on hold, then Foster was on the line, his voice guarded. "Chuikov? As in Colonel Peter Chuikov of the Spetsial'naya Naznacheniya?"

"The same, Colonel. Have you a moment and a secure line?"

"Depends on the nature of your call, Colonel. I didn't know you were in our country; are you on Bragg?"

Chuikov laughed. "No, no, I am not. You might say I'm standing out in the cold, looking for shelter. Can you suggest a place to stay?"

Tom Foster snapped his fingers loudly, the sound bringing his sergeant major into the office immediately. Motioning for the burly noncom to shut the door, Foster slid his bottom desk drawer open, flipping a silver toggle switch so that his conversation with the Russian officer was being both recorded and scrambled. "Go ahead, Peter. We're free to talk on this line but I am recording, and Sergeant Major Stump is in the office with me. Standard operating procedure, I hope you understand."

"I more than anyone," replied Chuikov. "It's not every day that a Spetsnaz officer calls and asks for help in defecting. You are well, my friend?"

"Fuck how I am, how are you? When did you arrive? Where are you now?" Foster checked himself in midflow, realizing the Russian would tell him what he could and reminding himself of the danger the man was putting himself in by remaining stationary. Should his people have discovered his defection, they would be looking for him with all available resources. The hunters' orders would be clear: kill Chuikov.

Chuikov scanned the mall parking lot; it was beginning to fill with early-morning shoppers. Several people had walked past him already, no one paying the lone caller any attention. Satisfied he was secure for the moment, Chuikov returned to his conversation. "I am fine. You may want to alert your FBI to speak with a young fisherman named Hobbs in Valdez. He gambles too much and spends more for cocaine than what a good season's fishing brings in. I enjoyed my ride across the water with him, though. A most gracious host and a fine boat as well."

"Got him. I'm sure the feds will be interested. Where are you now?" asked Foster.

"Anchorage. I drove up this morning. The weather is very good. I'm planning on doing some camping over the next few days. Maybe up around Fairbanks—do you know the area?"

"Sure. Rugged country up that way, Peter. How will we find you?"

A healthy young man in a red sports car pulled up alongside the curb, his sudden appearance causing the Russian to slip his hand around the Beretta's cool butt in preparation. "Hey! When's this place open up? They gotta record store?" he called from the car's dark rich interior.

Chuikov slipped the pistol's safety upward, hearing its muffled click as the weapon was armed. "I think they open in ten minutes," he offered. "Maybe a record store at the south end, I'm not sure.'' The man waved his thanks, slipping the expensive machine into gear, leaving with a sharp squeal from the tires as he sped off. Chuikov watched him park, then run across the lot and disappear into the building's southern entrance.

''Peter? You okay? Peter?'' Foster's voice held more than a hint of worry as he listened to the muffled exchange coming long distance across the line.

''*Da*? Yes, I'm fine. Where were we?''

Relieved, Tom Foster sat back in his chair, accepting a cigarette from Stump, who was now listening to the two men's conversation through the colonel's intercom. Blowing a long draft of smoke from his lungs, Foster replied. ''I need to know how to bring you in, and State will want to know why we should.''

Chuikov chuckled into the receiver. ''Ah, my first lesson in capitalism, no? With what will I buy my freedom? A good question to ask.''

At the other end Foster winced. ''Peter, you've been at this game at least as long as I have. You know those assholes at State will want something substantial for their efforts, and at the same time they'll be scratching their nuts wondering if you're not a plant. So help me get the ball rolling; what have you brought for us?''

Chuikov sighed. ''Stay where you are, I'll call from another phone in five minutes.'' Without waiting for an answer, the Spetsnaz colonel hung up, hurrying back to his car, not putting the Beretta on ''safe'' until the car was out of the parking lot.

Precisely five minutes had passed when Foster's phone rang again. In the meantime both the SOCOM colonel and his sergeant major had agreed to what needed to be done next. Stump was already making an appointment with their next-higher, a call to State next on his list. In the meantime Foster reviewed his personal file on Chuikov, whom he'd met several years before during an exercise in western Europe. At the time the Spetsnaz colonel had identified himself as a major with the Soviet Rocket Forces, an excellent cover, which Foster had only discovered after recognizing a picture of Chuikov taken in Afghanistan.

Foster's file was fairly complete, given what he'd been able to sift through from the different agencies whose records were available to him. The information he had was damned impressive. Colonel Peter Chuikov was a highly decorated Spetsnaz officer with known tours of duty in Vietnam, Rhodesia, Angola, Nicaragua, and most recently Afghanistan, where he'd been captured and held prisoner for three weeks until freed by a reinforced Spetsnaz team.

The CIA's records showed Chuikov as being suspected of engineering several high-level assassinations, including an American JUSMAG officer who was running a covert operation in Thailand for the United States. In addition to his battle prowess, the Soviet colonel was an accomplished athlete, having participated in two Olympic games, taking home a bronze and silver medal for his efforts. Most of the NSA's file notes were sketchy pertaining to Chuikov's shadowy appearance in Central America, where he had been training battalion-sized counterinsurgency units for the Sandinistas. At least one report verified Chuikov's presence in the field as an armed adviser.

After Afghanistan, Chuikov dropped out of sight and

was assumed to be on extended leave due to wounds received during his escape from rebel hands. Foster had gotten a short letter from the man several months ago, indicating he'd like to talk with the SOCOM officer in the near future. The letter had come through two cutouts inside friendly Third World embassies, whose military attachés were on speaking terms with Foster's office.

Damn! thought Foster as he lifted the receiver to his ear, if Chuikov's defection is sincere, we'll have scored a major coup against the Soviets. Especially if he brings out some hard intelligence on Spetsnaz activities in the West. Ensuring the scrambler was still activated, Foster cleared his throat and spoke.

Several blocks away from the mall, Chuikov glanced around as he waited for Foster to pick up on the line. He knew his use of the Valdez infiltration network would be reported by the fisherman who'd transported him, alerting Vasili Suworov of his whereabouts. It was certain the marshal would send a team after him, especially in light of what he'd taken to hand over to the Americans in exchange for asylum.

"Colonel Foster. Is this you, Peter?"

Chuikov smiled at the Green Beret officer's use of his first name, a tactic meant to encourage a relationship between the two men, which up until now was nonexistent except in the most professional of terms. "You wanted to know what I have brought to impress your State Department with, no? Listen closely, Tom. If you have a recorder operating—which I have no doubt you do—it will be most helpful."

For the next five minutes Chuikov described the package of materials he'd smuggled out of Moscow at the cost of a KGB agent who'd stumbled onto the Spetsnaz commando as he was preparing to leave from the Siberian coast for Valdez. "There you have it, Colonel. Do you think what I have to offer is worth your government's time and effort to continue this dialogue?"

In his office, the door locked, Colonel Tom Foster breathed out a long gust of pent-up air. The enormity of what Chuikov was claiming to possess had staggered him. If it was true, the United States would be in a position to close down at least three major spy networks operated by the Soviets in and around Alaska. In addition, State would possess a major trump card, which it could play whenever a power slam was necessary behind the scenes. Chuikov's information included every cache site and target folder associated with Spetsnaz activities and target sites in the forty-ninth state. From a strategic viewpoint, Alaska was critical to U.S. defense concerns, and it was well known in certain circles that the Russians had mounted small-force reconnaissance forays against selected military and civilian hard sites.

"I'll take what you've given me and have it transcribed, Colonel. Naturally I can't give you an answer at this point, that's State's prerogative. You'll need to contact us again, and we'll go from there."

Chuikov had expected this, and had planned for it. Turning to face the street, the Spetsnaz commander gently adjusted his Beretta so its butt wouldn't dig so deeply into the small of his back. It was a busy morning in the state's largest city, with cars and people beginning to fill up Fourth Avenue as businesses opened their doors. "Colonel Foster," began Chuikov, "I am not a hockey player wishing to join an American team, nor am I a ballet dancer looking for fame and fortune on the American stage. We both know what Spetsnaz is and how few of its people the West has seen defect.

"At this moment Vasili Suworov may be dispatching a team of my comrades to hunt me down. The orders will not include a reference to 'dead or alive,' only that I be located and the information I have be recovered. My death sentence was signed years ago when I was made a member of the wolf pack called Spetsnaz, and as is the habit of the wolf, we take care of our own.

"This afternoon I will FedEx a letter detailing where your people can expect to extract me. The method, time, and location will be fully described. I recommend you send your best, as Suworov will certainly send his. Tell your people at State they have one week at the most. After that . . . well, I know my brethren's zeal to accomplish Vasili's instructions."

For several moments the line was silent as both men considered their next moves. Chuikov was anxious to get on to the next phase of his plan, already knowing he was spending too much time in the open. Foster, realizing the Soviet colonel's plan would force State to bring him in, was considering what options he'd recommend to the general once State dropped the ball in their lap. The First Group at Lewis was the closest source of trained personnel, although the 10th possessed several mountain teams that could easily handle a recovery operation in the wilds of Alaska. He'd have to start doing some research right away, which meant letting Chuikov off the line.

"Peter, I'll pass your information and request to State immediately." Foster paused, hearing Stump's heavy thumping at his office door. "Do what you're going to, but be sure to address tomorrow's package 'personal/ confidential.' I know the danger you're in, and you've got my promise we'll do all we can to pull you in."

Chuikov grunted. Although Foster was a good man, he had little actual ground time as a Special Forces soldier. Tom Foster had no idea what the Russian was facing, for if he had, he'd have ordered Chuikov to the nearest military reservation and taken the responsibility on himself for the officer's safety. But Chuikov hadn't expected the offer, so he wasn't disappointed it hadn't materialized. "My appreciation for your time, Colonel. With luck, we'll see each other again in a week. If not . . ."

Foster heard the line go dead. Striding to the door, he let Stump in. "Well, what's the bastard got?" rumbled Stump, a fat cigar poking from between two thick lips.

"What he's got could shut down the Russians' efforts to gather intelligence and disrupt our defense systems in Alaska for years. But we've only got a week to field a team, locate the colonel, and extract him. Is the Old Man in?"

Stump pointed a dowel-sized index finger upward. "He's upstairs in the Green Room now. You've got his undivided attention for the next thirty minutes, then he's got to fly to Manila for a conference with the Commander-in-Chief, Pacific. I suggest you move your ass, sir."

Foster nodded, locking the scrambler's drawer and grabbing his hastily scribbled notes from the desk. "Thanks for getting me in, Sergeant Major. You might want to stand by. I have a feeling we're going to be pulling some overtime once this hits the fan."

"Overtime?" Stump growled from around the cigar's butt. "I'll be here when you get finished with the general, the wife'll understand. She's more SF than half the silly bastards around this place, anyway."

CHAPTER 2

Major Yuri Pushkin sucked in the smell of his own sweat, relishing its sour-sweet aroma. Peering through his binos, he watched the steady progression of the column of men below him as they trudged up a hill. It was the figure in the column's center that Pushkin was most interested in, primarily because he was the one Pushkin had been sent to kill.

A quick glance to his right confirmed Pushkin's spotter had also identified their target. The Spetsnaz commando was armed with a folding stock AK-74, as well as a bag of grenades and a heavy 9-mm automatic pistol. Strapped to his side was a long Nepalese kukri, its edge as sharp as a cat's whisker. Sergeant Antonov had worked with Pushkin for two years now and was closer to him than Yuri's own wife. ''You have him?'' asked the snakelike sergeant, his own binoculars glued to his face as he whispered.

Pushkin grunted. Carefully setting the expensive optic

down, he gingerly retrieved his custom-built sniper rifle from where it lay next to him, slipping the lightly oiled scope shroud free. The gun had been built by one of the Soviet Union's premier makers of such weapons. Unlike most Russian rifles, this one was chambered for NATO's 7.62 round, one that Pushkin favored for long-distance work. The heavy bullet in the barrel's chamber was as special as the rifle itself. Surrounded by a lightweight metal jacket, the 168-grain round had been cored, or hollowed, then filled with a mercury solution. The tip possessed a titanium nose cone, which was painted bright blue to separate it from standard 7.62 ammunition. Leaving the barrel at well over three thousand feet per second, the bullet was capable of boring itself through all but the thickest body armor before expanding to diameters of up to .71 caliber.

"It looks as if they are taking a break, Yuri," whispered Antonov. "Your target has placed his weapon on the ground and is now taking pictures."

Pushkin eased the desert-colored fiberglass stock into the deep pocket of his shoulder. Arching his neck, he then slid his whiskered cheek along the smooth rifle butt, aware from long hours behind the gun of his stock weld, once he'd reached it. His callused hand wrapped around the profiled comb, the Russian gently lay his trigger finger alongside the safety lever located just forward of the trigger itself. With one easy motion Pushkin could release the safety, pull the trigger, then place the weapon back on safe. The rifle was an auto-loader, capable of utilizing either five-, ten-, or twenty-round box magazines, which were carried in a special nylon harness worn by the sniper. There were only three other guns like

Pushkin's in the Spetsnaz inventory, each assigned to an interdiction specialist who had proved himself worthy of being awarded sole access to his particular weapon.

Peering through the 10X scope, he found the tall journalist easily as the man moved among the resting guerrillas. Pushkin grunted at Antonov, who quickly slipped a heavy lump of reddish wax beneath the rifle's forestock so that it formed a smooth platform on which the rifle could be swiveled back and forth. In an emergency the wax could be eaten. Yuri grimaced as he remembered the only occasion he'd had to test his survival instructor's theory about the wax. His gut grumbled in protest as it, too, recalled attempting to digest the oily mess.

Adjusting the rifle, Pushkin made a slight body adjustment, then checked the sun's location. Satisfied there would be no telltale glint off the highly polished scope lens, he began willing himself to physically "melt" into the gun, becoming one with it. The American reporter-of-fortune was busy chatting with his companions now, a long-barreled camera dangling loosely around his neck. Slowly twisting the adjustment ring, Yuri brought the man into perfect focus, his image in sharp relief against the hard yellow background of the sun-blasted rocks behind him.

"Yuri?"

"Soon, Antonov. I need the proper angle."

A brutal smile ripped across the Russian noncom's craggy features. He understood what angle the major was seeking, having lain by his side on more than a few outings such as this. Pushkin delighted in not just killing his assigned targets, but in blowing their heads off. The blue-tipped partition round was fully capable of accomplishing this if placed an inch behind the lower jaw's hinge point, just under the base of the skull. Antonov recalled watching several of Pushkin's unwary targets' heads pop like corks under pressure as the high-velocity bullet struck them. He, for one, found this highly amusing. "Our wordsmith has written his last 'revelation' for the world press, eh, Yuri?"

"Without a doubt, old friend," replied Pushkin as he eased the safety lever forward. The reporter had become a thorn in the Soviet high command's side, his stories of Third World combat involving Russian interests having ignited Western outrage on a frequent basis. A former Special Forces soldier in the American army, the writer had on many occasions shot more than just pictures during his forays into places like Nicaragua, Angola, Chad, Lebanon, and now Afghanistan. The order had been given. Spetsnaz had been sent. The bullet with the journalist's name on it was seconds away from being fired, its journey suspended only until the proper angle presented itself to the patient gunman hidden well over three hundred meters from where the group was now posing for one final portrait.

As usual, Pushkin didn't realize he'd pulled the trigger until the heavy crack of the rifle jolted him out of his trance. He watched with professional satisfaction as the round penetrated the man's deeply tanned skin, striking precisely one inch behind his pronounced jawbone. A millisecond later the partition bullet welled up inside the journalist's neck; a massive transformation of kinetic energy exploded fragile tissues in a thunderclap of bloody spray and rendered flesh. The major grunted involuntarily as he observed the man's head shooting skyward like a hairy comet in flight. The body itself sank to its knees, a crimson column of shattered spinal cord poking up like a splintered signpost from inside the man's well-worn battle tunic. Slowly, like an ancient tree whose roots had rotted away until they could no longer bear the trunk's stupendous weight, the corpse fell forward, landing with a heavy thump amid the suddenly frenzied Afghan rebels.

"Fire!" screamed Antonov, whose own AK-74 was already pumping a steady stream of tiny 5.54 tumblers downrange at the scattering guerrillas. On either side of the two men, weapons erupted. The sodden pop of a Spetsnaz grenade launcher caused Pushkin to lower his head: the detonation seconds later brought a gut-wrenching scream from the rocks below. The rapid staccato of their own RPD light machine gun was answered by one from the Afghan side of the house, its gunner desperately attempting to lay down a base of fire so that his comrades could break contact.

"Nikolai, the gun! Blow that bastard to hell!" Responding to his sergeant's order, the Spetsnaz grenadier took careful aim despite the whine of whistling steel. The resulting *crummp* threw bits of fragmented metal high in the air; a stunned freedom fighter staggered out into the open, his hands clenched tightly around his bleeding middle. A cross-fire of tracer and steel took him apart at the knees and chest.

Suddenly a man broke from cover, running a zigzag pattern towards the safety of a jumble of huge boulders. Pushkin leaped to his feet, bringing the custom autoloader up in the classic offhand position and snapping a hastily aimed shot at the fleeing rebel's back. "Get down, you crazy fool!'' ordered Antonov, whose beefy hand was already jerking the officer off his feet. ''I don't want to explain to our boss how I let Mother Russia's best Spetsnaz officer get his stupid ass shot off by a raghead while I was supposed to be watching him,'' growled the sweating sergeant.

Rolling over on his back, Pushkin laughed out loud at his friend's admonition. He'd been wounded five times during his career as a Spetsnaz officer, once almost dying before his men had gotten him to their emergency extraction point. I should request a staff job, he thought as a long burst from an American-made M-16 ripped over their position. One day the good Sergeant Antonov won't be around to pull my nuts out of the fire and then where will I be?

''By the way, you got the silly asshole!'' yelled Antonov. ''Flipped him like a coin. Damn impressive shot for an officer.''

Rolling onto his belly, Pushkin slapped the battle-wise noncom hard on his beefy shoulder. ''Let's get the hell out of here,'' he roared so as to be heard above the continuing gunfire. ''We've done what we were sent to do.''

Antonov nodded, pulling a stubby black flare pistol from its holster. Aiming high in the air, he abruptly spotted a rebel who had worked himself up along their right flank during the firefight and was taking aim at the burly sergeant himself. With a curse Antonov dropped into a crouch, clutching the flare gun between his two huge fists and firing just as the Afghan pulled his own trigger.

A high-pressure spray of blood erupted from the Spetsnaz sergeant's left shoulder as the freedom fighter's quickly aimed bullet clipped through it, exiting cleanly but center-punching the grenadier who was shrugging into his rucksack behind Antonov. The Afghan's head vented itself of brain matter as Antonov's flare fused to his skull. The Spetsnaz team watched the body drop from sight back into the natural trench where the man had hidden, phosphorus steam rising upward as the body continued to cook.

"Destroy our comrade's body," ordered Pushkin. "These dogs must not have it for their barbaric rites of revenge." Turning to Antonov, who was busily binding his wound, Pushkin asked him how bad it was.

"A gnat's nibble, that's all," replied the veteran commando. "I've suffered worse from the clap." Jerking the bandage's knot tight, Antonov retrieved his assault rifle from where it had fallen. Finding the magazine nearly empty, he slipped it from the weapon's well and inserted a fresh box, jerking the rifle's charging bolt to the rear with a loud clack.

One of the three remaining commandos finished putting an antipersonnel mine beneath the body of their fallen companion. With a nod from Pushkin, the man carefully tugged the safety clip free from its housing, arming the mine. Whoever turned the corpse over to loot it would find himself staring at five hundred steel balls traveling at well over fifteen hundred feet per second, courtesy of the Soviet Union. "Let's go," ordered Pushkin.

Cautiously the team began leapfrogging to their rear, weapons at the ready should anyone be foolish enough to want to continue the fight. As they entered a narrow crack in the hillside, which led to the plateau high above the ambush site, Pushkin caught the brief reflection of the sun off the dead journalist's camera lens, the effect startling him. With a snarl he raised the sniper rifle to his shoulder one last time, blowing the expensive camera apart before slipping into the rocky aperture's womb behind his men's retreating figures.

CHAPTER 3

Lieutenant Commander Paul Kinder watched intently as the powerfully built man wearing a pair of SEAL running boots, faded Levis, and a tight-fitting black tank top stepped up to the firing line. In his hands he held a cut-down 12-gauge shotgun, its speed sling looped across his thick chest to give the weapon stability during rapid firing. Less than ten yards to his front stood three metal targets, their surfaces dented from the impact of hundreds of steel pellets over the course of the last week's training. A hand grenade simulator suddenly exploded off to the man's left flank, its sound signaling the beginning of the firearms course for Beaumont ''Bo'' Thornton.

Kinder observed Thornton's reaction to the simulator as he flawlessly emptied the shotgun's tubular magazine into the hinged metal silhouettes, knocking each down with two blasts of number-four buck apiece. Dropping the weapon at his feet, Thornton sprinted up a narrow dirt path, stopping fifty meters uphill at a table, where a disassembled Glock 19 lay. As Bo effortlessly slapped the pistol together, ramming the plus-two magazine up the Glock's vacant well and letting the slide fly forward to chamber a round, the Navy special warfare officer couldn't help but be impressed. For the last two weeks Thornton, Frank Hartung, and Jason Silver had been "guests" of the Special Warfare Center at Coronado Island. Their attendance had been approved by a high Pentagon source whose message came through Admiral Benson's office at SpecWar Command, just up the street from the center. Kinder knew both Thornton and Hartung were retired Green Berets whose dive shop across the bay was a favorite hangout for many of the SEALs from Teams 1, 3, and 5. The lieutenant commander wasn't familiar with the third man of the group, a small fellow who carried a deep scar across his lower belly and possessed an almost magical knack for blowing things up. The SEAL officer nodded to himself as Thornton double-tapped six successive targets with the Glock, dropping it to the ground and heading for the next station at a run.

"Who do you think these guys are, sir?" The speaker, a heavily muscled ensign from SEAL Team 3, had stepped up beside Kinder without the officer sensing his presence until they were standing shoulder to shoulder.

"Beats me, Sam. I thought Thornton and Hartung were retired, but NavCom's message from D.C. would indicate otherwise."

Sam, who was a legend in the teams for one particular exploit against the Libyans during a midnight reconnaissance of their coast, shrugged. "If they're 'retired,' then I'm a black-shoe sailor. I've never heard of San Clemente being roped off so a coupla old-timers could pop caps and play with an SDV for two weeks. Plus, look at the instructors who're here. Every swinging dick has a Q clearance. These are guys who don't write their mothers anymore, much less blab out of school about what they do. These boys must be pretty high speed to rate this kind of attention."

Kinder absently nodded in concurrence. San Clemente lay nearly sixty miles off the California coastline. It was a rugged stretch of ground, used by the Special Warfare Center and SEAL teams to conduct land warfare and small-arms training. Normally there would be a class of BUDs, or SEAL students, going through their second phase of instruction on the island. That schedule had been modified to accommodate the Pentagon's request to requalify the three "civilians" in the latest small-arms SEAL delivery vehicle (SDV), and Low-Altitude–Low-Opening (LALO) techniques being perfected by the Navy for its SpecWar operatives. Since the Heavy Hook dive shop was in San Diego, it had been determined that the Navy's Amphibious School at Coronado would serve as the Springblade team's training facility whenever they needed an upgrade or introduction to what was new in the field of special ops.

Kinder just couldn't figure out who had determined this, since it seemed to fly in the face of the Navy's passion for secrecy about its special-warfare capabilities. "Whatever they're hooked into, they're damn good. Hartung and Thornton worked joint ops with us in Vietnam, and Master Chief Kruger tells me our Mr. Silver did two tours with the Rangers in Southeast Asia. Our orders are to provide them with whatever they need, and we can pull from any inventory in SOCOM to do it."

Both men watched as Thornton prepared to finish the combat course. The tall commando had just finished negotiating a series of obstacles during which he'd engaged nine different hostage situations using a Beretta 92 and an Uzi SMG. Handing the weapons off to a SEAL instructor standing close by, Thornton clambered up a fifty-foot rope ladder leading to a wooden platform suspended high above the ground. Once on top, he hooked into a rappel seat and descended at high speed onto the top of a mock-up of a fuselage of a 737 airliner. Dancing down the length of the plane, Bo found a Minimi LMG waiting for him near the tail. Hoisting the weapon, Thornton charged it and began laying down a base of fire for Hartung and Silver, who were just leaving their own lanes of fire. As the two men scrambled forward toward a squat concrete bunker, Bo tore up two groups of cardboard targets representing terrorist infantry. Seeing Silver's ass disappear inside the structure, Thornton hooked a length of perlon rope to a ring bolted to the mock-up's frame and slid downward to the ground. From inside the bunker came the high-pitched cough of a recoilless rifle being fired as both Hartung and Silver lined up on a derelict minivan four hundred meters to their front. As the SEALs watched in professional admiration, the van exploded under the impact of the first round, shaking mightily on its shredded wheels as a second round blew out its side.

Twenty-five meters to its right flank, a host of steel pop-up targets erupted into view. Thornton slipped the Minimi from its sling and, hugging its stock tightly against his right hip, began sending long, stinging bursts of .223 fire into their ranks. Target after target dropped from view until all that was left was an open lane to the sea. Standing on the fuselage above the sweating warrior, Kinder turned to his ensign. "If these sons of bitches are retired, I wonder what it would take to get them back on active duty! I haven't seen this caliber of teamwork since we were operating in the Rung Sat. These guys look more like SEALs than Army pukes."

Laughing, Sam threw a quick salute down to Thornton, who'd overheard the SEAL officer's comment as he finished clearing the smoking Minimi's chamber. "Commander, I don't know who these dudes are with now, but from what they've shown us these last two weeks I sure wouldn't mind teaming up with them myself. We're bad, but those boys down there are *baaaaad* to the bone . . . and that's no shit."

The two sailors watched as Hartung and Silver climbed out of the bunker, huge smiles on their faces as they spotted Thornton's lanky figure heading toward them. When all three men met, they exchanged handshakes and high-fives, their good-natured catcalls echoed by the SEAL cadre, which was beginning to join them. Suddenly one of the SEALs pointed skyward toward a dark shadow that streaked over the group, its rotors whining at high speed in the heavy ocean air. "Chopper coming in!" the Navy commando announced.

Hartung, a sodden sweatband tied around his head, glanced briefly at the descending aircraft, then turned his attention to Thornton, who was casually flipping his Russian-made ballistic knife end over end in his hand. "Why do I get the feeling that chopper's for us?" asked the veteran of three wars.

"Instinct, you old bastard. We came out by sea, supposed to go back to SpecWar the same way. Kinder's people have a radio link, so this has to be something special . . . and that might mean Calvin's onto something for us.''

''I fucking-A hope so,'' chimed in Silver. ''All this 'rest and relaxation' is killing me. A good contract would come in handy, given what its costing to open my art gallery in Seaside.''

Frank Hartung grabbed the compact former Ranger around the throat, pretending to throttle him. ''Art gallery? What the hell does a lowlife like you know about art?''

Silver quickly broke the sergeant major's halfhearted hold, stepping back out of reach as Thornton waved to the pilot, stepping clear of the loach's doorless cockpit. ''I don't know shit about art, but Linda says most of the assholes who buy it are in the same boat. After she gets Bo's house furnished she's going to get me squared away with a business like you two retreads. God knows I won't be able to hump a ruck forever.''

''Let's go see Calvin,'' invited Bo. ''Looks like we've been activated again.''

''Kinder tells me you boys have been kicking ass, not that I expected anything less.'' Calvin Bailey expertly popped the top from an ice-cold can of Coors, draining half the beer in one long swallow. The DEA agent who was Springblade's link between the president and a small circle of advisers sat atop a crate of 203 ammunition, his leather flight jacket off, revealing a well-used S&W Model 19 .357 Magnum in an Alessi shoulder holster.

Silver fished a beer from the cooler at his feet, emptying it over his head and down his neck. "Yeah!" he hooted. "It's Miller time and now that Calvin 'I'm so secret I'll have to kill ya' Bailey is here, we can party hardy!"

Thornton, a canteen of Gatorade in his hand, finished thanking Kinder's people for their efforts and watched as they trooped down to the beach, where three Seafox open-ocean assault boats waited to transport them back to Coronado. Three of the SEALs would be staying on the island, packaging weapons and cleaning up until a CH-53 came out for them. Good people, Bo thought to himself. Professional as hell, yet totally unassuming in every respect. Thornton had always enjoyed working with the SEALs, recalling the time he'd spent on Okinawa running the joint Army-Navy SCUBA program during Vietnam.

Sauntering over to where his own team sat waiting, Bo Thornton wondered what Calvin Bailey found so important that he would fly out from D.C. It had been nearly two months since Bo and David Lee, the team's only active-duty member, had inserted into Nicaragua to track down a renegade Green Beret whose misguided patriotism to his native land might have cost the United States its precious toehold in Central America. Lee was still recovering from his wounds at Bragg, splitting his time between the hospital and the SERE committee's RTL out at Camp Rowe, where he was acting First Sergeant. Thornton had spent most of his time finishing the house he and Linda were building on the Oregon coast.

It had been Conrad Billings's idea to send the three men to Coronado for some hands-on training, and Bo was thankful for the opportunity, as it gave him a chance to check in on Heavy Hook's progress. Hartung was showing a six-figure gross on the books, which was staggering to Thornton, since he'd been gone from San Diego ever since Springblade became a reality. "You just give the people what they want," explained Frank to him over dinner his first night in town. "We're doing underwater photography classes, recreational-diving, delivery systems, specialty classes like shark hunting, the whole nine yards. I got fourteen instructors on the payroll, half of them real-deal, moonlighting SEALs. Heavy Hook's so far in the black we ought to be consultants on the economy."

Jason Silver, the team's demolitions expert, had been ecstatic over the opportunity to exchange information with the Navy's spec-war specialists on the latest explosives. Living just up the highway from Thornton, Jason was carving his own niche in the business community by opening an art gallery. Silver had worked with Thornton in Vietnam, finding volunteers for Bo's "Krieg" project and furnishing information and equipment whenever something special was needed in a hurry. He'd moved to Oregon after the team's first successful mission, finding a new purpose to his life after years of postwar frustration. It was Silver who handled the logistics when Springblade went into action, a task no one envied, given the complexity of their missions.

". . . so it looks like SF is going to start running hot missions in those countries I mentioned, unless the Marine Corps convinces everybody they can do the job better. The DEA's hands are full just trying to tread water inside our own borders without having to play 'Roland the Headless Thompson Gunner' in Peru and elsewhere." Bailey, crushing the now-empty beer can, grabbed another and offered Thornton a crate as he joined them.

Looking at the faces around him, Bo asked the question that was by right his to present. "So, Calvin, what brings you to our island?"

Laughter rippled through the group as Bailey flipped his friend a one-finger salute. "Kinder told me you guys kicked butt out here, which is quite a compliment coming from a SEAL about Army assholes. Billings gives his regards and asked me to tell you the president is extremely happy with this project. Three missions out of the hat and all of them successful; not a bad average, given our previous scores on the Special Ops board.

"Lee's recovering nicely, although he took Colonel Rowe's assassination pretty hard. We expect he'll be up to snuff physically in another month or so."

"That's good news, squid," barked Hartung. "Now, what's the story with you and the chopper? Tell us something we don't know."

Bailey let fly with a long gut-wrenching belch in Hartung's direction. "Still the same old lovable grandfather type, eh, Frank? Anyhow, Conrad attended an emergency meeting with the president yesterday. Seems we've got a Spetsnaz colonel who has infiltrated into Alaska using a KGB-Spetsnaz network we were unaware of until his call. Our boy wants to defect, and is willing to buy his citizenship with some very interesting information, which we believe he's brought out with him. State as well as the Pentagon wants Colonel Chuikov recovered, and the president wants Springblade to pull the mission."

"When are we expected to launch?" asked Thornton.

"The four of us are booked civilian into Anchorage. We'll be met by some folks from Air Force pararescue and work out of their shop. I gave Kinder a list of gear we'll need. Anything else, Silver can lock in to between now and mission launch."

Thornton reached into the half-full cooler, pulling back the first beer he'd had since arriving on San Clemente. Opening it, he raised his hand in a toast. "Cheers, gentlemen. It looks like we're back in business."

"Airborne and amen," agreed Hartung.

"Your momma," burped Calvin Bailey as the CH-53, which would move the team back to the SpecWar Center, began its approach toward the island.

As one they moved toward the remaining SEALs to help load out.

CHAPTER 4

Chuikov parked the car on Fourth Avenue, locking its doors more as an excuse to survey the sidewalks and street for KGB tails than out of concern for the automobile. Satisfied he was of no more interest to the shoppers than normal, he trotted across traffic and headed toward the Captain Cook Hotel several blocks away. He would be moving quite a bit around Anchorage over the next twenty-four hours, and it seemed a good idea to leave the car in different locations as a security precaution. Chuikov possessed survival instincts that had been honed under the most oppressive conditions. He was not paranoid; he was a survivor in the healthiest meaning of the term.

Entering the plush hotel's lobby, he quickly checked his box for messages, avoiding an unnecessary verbal exchange with the lovely young clerk. If there were any telephone messages, which there should not be, he would find out once he reached his room. Strolling across the lobby and into the small gift shop kitty-corner to the hotel entrance, Chuikov made a quick visual recon of the people milling around the hotel's main floor. Again satisfied he wasn't being waited for or followed, the Russian commando took the elevator to his room on the fourteenth floor.

After a cursory inspection of the room, Chuikov lay down on the freshly made bed and began thumbing through a Brigade Quartermaster catalog he'd picked up earlier in his travels. He needed equipment that would allow him to camp and forage comfortably for a maximum of ten days in the Alaskan wilds, and he needed it quickly. After several minutes of note making, he dialed the company's 1–800 number and gave his order along with a major credit-card number, which would draw funds from a Spetsnaz account on a bank in Anchorage. Requesting overnight delivery to the hotel he would be staying at for one night in Fairbanks, Chuikov chuckled to himself, thinking how Suworov would react when he got the bill.

A second phone call to a local gun store immediately netted him both a compact 12-gauge shotgun and a Ruger M77 .223 hunting rifle with scope. For these he would pay cash, promising to be at the store just before it closed that afternoon. Chuikov went on to order 250 rounds of number-four buck for the pump gun, with 100 rounds of hunting ammunition for the Ruger. America was a great country, he thought out loud. Where else could the average citizen arm himself with one phone call and a handful of cash? Certainly not in Russia or communist China, countries that frowned on their people having the means to defend themselves against internal as well as external enemies.

With logistics well in hand, Chuikov turned his attention to the question of transportation. As it was, he planned to take the train that ran daily between Anchorage and Fairbanks, leaving early in the morning with a noon arrival. From there he would check into the Golden Nugget, retrieve his outdoor equipment, then contact one of the several bush pilots who flew out of the state's northernmost city. In less than forty-eight hours Colonel Peter Chuikov would be safely hidden away in the virgin wilderness of Alaska's Brooks Range, dependent only on his own skills and cunning until whoever Foster's government sent to extract him made contact. At the same time he reminded himself of Vasili Suworov's rage and determination to reach him first, knowing a Spetsnaz team was most likely already preparing to cross the Bering Sea in pursuit.

Checking his watch, a gift from a now-dead Russian premier for his services in Angola and Chad, Chuikov noted he had several hours to kill before meeting the sporting-goods store owner. Slipping the Beretta from inside his waistband, he ejected the magazine, leaving a single round in the chamber just in case. Unloading all three clips, Chuikov checked their spring tension and floor plates. Reloading the automatic, he flicked the safety off, placing the pistol within hand's reach on the bed.

Switching on the television, Chuikov dialed his way through the channels to the news. He was addicted to the CNN network. After two stories on toxic waste, one on an airliner that had plowed through a school yard in

Texas, and an interview with an aging rock musician who was going on the road one more time, Chuikov's attention was riveted to the screen as the rugged hills of Afghanistan came on his set.

Within three minutes the Russian colonel knew all he needed to about the death of the American journalist at the hands of unknown assassins two days before. The mission profile was familiar to Chuikov, primarily because he had been part of the think tank that had planned the man's death six months before the team headed by Major Pushkin had been deployed. The CNN reporter alluded to rumors of rival Afghan factions warring between each other as being the root of the fatal ambush. Chuikov could have rocketed her career skyward had he been so inclined. The KGB wanted the meddlesome reporter dead, and Spetsnaz had done the job as part of a larger operation meant to eliminate the most influential members of the resistance movement, thereby plunging the country into a violent civil war for years to come. Hussein and Mullah Woodud had also been on Pushkin's list, but Gulbuddin Hekhmatyar's *mujahedin* had gotten to the popular guerrilla leaders first. Chuikov suspected it had been Pushkin who'd also engineered the murder of the American Special Forces colonel in Manila; it was the man's style.

Snapping the set off, Chuikov considered these most recent developments and what they might mean. Pushkin was an up-and-comer in Spetsnaz, a soldier with few equals among his peers, a man who was known to be fond of striking against American targets. Would Suworov send him to America? It seemed likely, there was no love shared between Chuikov and Pushkin, whose teams had enjoyed a bitter competition for years. The Russian lay back on the comfortable bed, his hand absently touching the Beretta as if to assure itself the gun was still there. If Pushkin was available, Vasili would send him.

Within minutes Chuikov was fast asleep, sure in the knowledge he was now a wolf whose own pack would devour him if they could bring him to bay. Time was now of the essence, as was rest.

Outside it began to rain.

CHAPTER 5

"We know the colonel is in Anchorage as of yesterday. There is no doubt he has contacted someone in the American government, who must now decide the worth of extending political asylum to a defecting Spetsnaz officer. It will take time to evaluate the intelligence Chuikov has dishonored himself by taking from us, time which I intend to use to find him and—"

"Kill him?"

"Yes. Of course."

Pushkin gazed across Suworov's massive desktop, hoping he was containing the jolt of adrenaline that had just coursed through his system like a dirty burst of electricity. He'd been transported by fighter ahead of Antonov and the rest of the team, reaching Moscow in the early hours of the morning. Pushkin knew he looked like shit. The mission had been long and extremely taxing, both mentally and physically. The reporter's death had signaled its end, a HIP swooping down to extract the

Spetsnaz commandos once they'd gained the high ground above the ambush site. They'd all hoped for some stand-down time; instead Suworov's orders had brought him to the heart of Mother Russia within hours.

"When do we leave?" he asked.

Suworov grunted with satisfaction. He'd known the major would accept the challenge in spite of just coming out of the field. The Russian special forces commander had read the initial reports from the KGB's field agents in Afghanistan, all of which confirmed the effectiveness of Pushkin's efforts to eradicate the *mujahedin* leadership's central core. Twelve targets had been identified, seven located and engaged successfully, to include the American journalist. It was a worthy achievement by anyone's standards, he mused to himself. "Tomorrow morning. Will your men be capable of extending themselves for this, or would you like a new team?"

Pushkin waved a hand in front of him, as if sweeping Suworov's concerns away. "*Nyet*. We lost two men who can be replaced. I'd like to draw them from Igor Pavlovovitch's team if they are available."

Suworov nodded his assent. "Your equipment and funds have been prepared and await you on the coast. Infiltration will be by sea, with one of our agents on the mainland transporting you to Anchorage by road. It is my belief, knowing Colonel Chuikov as I do, that he will not stay long in the city.

"Our colonel has no illusions as to how the Americans may or may not react to him. He will position himself so as to take advantage of the greatest number of options available, of which there are few. If he stays in the city he is at grave risk from both sides. On the other hand, should he retreat into the mountains, he continues to control his own destiny."

"How so?" invited Pushkin.

Vasili Suworov stood, gracefully stretching himself. He'd been in his office for over eighteen hours now, allowing himself only a brief nap prior to the young major's arrival from Afghanistan. Crossing the wide floor, he indicated with a nod the pot of American coffee sitting on a low table in the office's far corner. Pushkin rose in acceptance, his body needing something to sustain it after the long flight from Kabul. Both men exchanged small talk as they filled their generous Russian cups. Suworov answered the major's last question while watching the emerging sun burning away the morning's mist from Red Square.

"A man such as Chuikov could sustain himself indefinitely if he reached the mountains at this time of year. We know he has planned his moves carefully over a period of time, taking what he's needed to buy and bargain himself into his current position. Colonel Chuikov will not trust his fate to the wisdom of the American intelligence community this early in the game. He will want them to demonstrate their sincerity, which means he will force them to make a bold move, a move which will commit them to him.

"It is my belief he will go to the mountains, probably somewhere above Fairbanks, to await an American extraction team. We know he took with him at least one transponder, which could signal a plane as to his location. He has money, credit-card numbers, and several contacts within the SOCOM community at Fort Bragg and in Washington itself. If worse were to come to worse, our colonel could simply choose to disappear, making his way to Canada over a period of time."

Setting his coffee cup down, the Spetsnaz CinC turned and faced Pushkin, who was once again seated in front of his desk. "You will meet with one of our agents who spotted Chuikov earlier in Anchorage, and has traced his rental car to a 'Mr. Tom Jones.' Your man is currently checking every major hotel for a guest using this name, although I believe the colonel will be gone by the time your team arrives.

"Chuikov knows we will find him sooner or later. Spetsnaz operating procedures are specific in cases such as these, and he is using what he has been trained to do just as we will use the same techniques to catch wind of his trail. His advantage lies in moving quickly into a position he can defend or abandon. It should be an interesting chase for you, Major."

"My team . . ." began Pushkin.

"Arrives by noon today," finished Suworov. "I have ordered a quick medical exam as well as some 'entertainment' so as to relax them before you leave. Tell me who you want from Captain Pavlovovitch's team, and I will order them detached. By tomorrow night you will be on American soil and in pursuit of a man I never would have suspected of betraying his country or uniform. I wish you and your men good hunting."

Pushkin rose, knowing the interview was over, that he was free to leave and get some rest before Antonov and the others arrived. "Sir," he asked. "Is there a price we must pay if we fail?"

Suworov pursed his lips, hands clasped behind his back in a pose he'd made famous during the war against

Hitler years before. "A price? No, not in this case. On the other hand, though, there is a great reward awaiting you and your men should they succeed in running this renegade to ground. Remember you are Spetsnaz, Major Pushkin. In Spetsnaz we assign only the most difficult tasks, those which are considered impossible to accomplish by forces lesser than ourselves. I am not interested in 'failure,' only in the extent of how successful our efforts prove to be.

"If you manage to kill Chuikov, and of all my wolves you alone have the greatest possibility of doing so, I can promise you a comfortable career from this point on. On the other hand, my simply sending your team after this traitor will convey a message to any others within Spetsnaz who might entertain similar notions in the future. We will not tolerate betrayal within our ranks. I will snuff it out using any means regardless of cost!

"Go now, get some rest. My orderly will awaken you once it is time to rejoin your men."

Pushkin watched as Suworov turned to the window, its panes beginning to warm in the soft glow of the day. Without a sound the major left his seat, striding with a purpose to the open door, where a Spetsnaz escort awaited him. Once away from the office, Pushkin wondered whether he should congratulate or condemn himself for his selection as the man to hunt Chuikov down. He had no love for Chuikov, despite professional admiration for what had been up until now a splendid reputation. There was no better team to field than Pushkin's. They were in good health despite the trek through Afghanistan's moonlike terrain, and they functioned together as a well-oiled machine. The two men whose names he'd left on Suworov's desk would fit in easily, both having served with Antonov previously.

"Your quarters, Comrade Major."

With a start, Pushkin realized he'd been merely following his guide through the hallways of the command center, oblivious to where he was being led. I'm more tired than I thought, he confirmed to himself, entering the comfortable room and shutting the door. As he lay down and began to drift into what would be a deep sleep, Pushkin realized the enormity of their undertaking. An interdiction mission *within* the United States itself! He'd never heard of such a mission, even though Spetsnaz trained for such things on a regular basis. Blowing Colonel Chuikov's head off would be a pleasure, he decided. Doing it in America, on the other hand, would be an honor.

As Pushkin slept two floors below Suworov's office, an accountant in the KGB's international finance office received a curious message from a blind fund in the United States. Confirming the account number, he then checked it against known operations being conducted in the area for use authorization. Discovering there were no such ops being run by Suworov's people, the accountant immediately notified his supervisor, who in turn called the general's office.

Minutes later Vasili Suworov was advised that someone was tampering with Spetsnaz funds in Alaska. Ordering more coffee, the general congratulated himself on being handed another piece of the puzzle confronting him. Soon they would be within striking distance of Chuikov; soon they would put the man's head in his own hands as a lesson to all.

CHAPTER 6

Thornton knew he was asleep. The former Green Beret was as sure of this fact as he was of where he and the rest of the team were at the very moment the dream began. Beside him in first class sat Frank Hartung, a plastic glass of iced whiskey in his hand and a battered news magazine in his lap. One row over were Calvin Bailey and Jason Silver, both engrossed in a game of chess they had been playing ever since the flight left LAX two hours earlier. Thornton knew where he was, but the dream came anyway.

The birds and insects continued their chatter even as the point man slowly pushed his blackened hand upward sinking to one knee as he did so. Behind him the rest of team's stubby black barrels swung outward to cover their flanks, sweating bodies lowering like compressed springs onto the jungle's hard-packed floor. No one spoke. Instead, eyes and ears began sorting through thousands of bits of information presented to them.

T.I. Jackson had heard or seen *something*, and the veteran SOG point rarely missed a beat when he was up front as scout.

The rapid-fire, singsong rhythm of Vietnamese voices threaded its way through the jungle's other sounds, touching sensitive chords in the patrol's combat consciousness, which began vibrating like a suddenly hammered brass gong. Fingers tightened around pistol grips and forestocks, thumbs steadying themselves atop well-oiled safety levers in nervous anticipation of what was to come. The owners of the chattering voices were close by, their words as distinct as their northern accents. Someone dropped a tin pan or canteen, the others laughing, at his clumsiness. The burning smell of crude tobacco caused the tiger-striped commandos' noses to wrinkle in recognition of Chinese-made cigarettes, smokes normally found only in the rucksacks and pockets of North Vietnamese regulars.

T.I.'s head rotated slowly rearward until his eyes locked on those of the team leader's. Thornton nodded just a fraction, telling his point man to move ahead until they'd made eye contact with whoever was just meters away. Behind Thornton were three other men, one American new to SOG and two Nung mercenaries. RT Python had been on the ground for a week, tapping NVA communication lines and taking pictures of Russian-made 40mm antiaircraft guns for the Air Force to either bomb or avoid. The team had just slipped across a series of small streams that fed a river flowing south when T.I.'s senses picked up the enemy. Everyone wanted to avoid contact if at all possible, which was their mission, anyway. "Strictly a reconnaissance operation," was what

Major Dunderson had told the men at the end of their briefing at CCN's heavily fortified base camp. "Gather whatever information you can about what the dinks have built up in the area and bring it home. Command has purposely left the NVA alone there for nearly two months now, so their guard will be down. Avoid contact at all costs; you're going to have to hump at least a klick or two away before an extraction chopper can risk pulling you out."

After two days on the ground Thornton understood why. The NVA had reopened one of their tunnel complexes that had been dug years before during the French-Indo-china war. Swarms of intense young men were attending to camouflage, fortifications, communications bunkers, and guard duty. The RT found three radar-controlled antiaircraft batteries, photographing them and committing their coordinates to memory. Thornton was amazed at the size of the base, estimating at least two thousand NVA. Twice they'd nearly been discovered, and twice they'd squeezed out within seconds and inches of being melted down in a cross fire of enemy steel. A lesser team might have been lost, but Thornton's was made up of the best and most seasoned recon artists CCN had. Now it was just a matter of avoiding one more confrontation, and they'd be on their way home.

On hands and knees now, the team crawled through the jungle. Jackson carefully cleared a path for the others to follow, removing sharp bits of wood and rock from his newly broken path, bending wait-a-minute vines back and intertwining them with others so that they wouldn't catch on the men behind him. Jackson was a full-blooded Apache who'd joined the Army to escape reservation life. He'd been a natural for Special Forces, graduating from Bragg to Vietnam to SOG on the basis of an outstanding attitude and inbred ability to wage the kind of warfare SF prided itself on. T. I. was short for "The Indian," a nickname given the Apache warrior by Sergeant Major Flossom in training group at Bragg.

He'd been Thornton's point for several months now, having extended his tour, and transferred to CCN from CCC because "things were too slow for me there." Jackson wore his otter-black hair long by Army standards and carried one of the rare Special Forces tomahawks that had been issued to the first Hatchet teams formed. Stitched into the narrow brim of his well-worn boonie hat was a beaded image of a stalking cougar, as well as several of his tribe's most sacred symbols. Thornton knew Jackson to have counted coup, or touched the living bodies of his enemies, on at least two occasions before killing them. The Apache was combat cautious, yet as cool under fire as any man Bo had ever served with, and he was now signaling a second halt with just the barest flicker of a finger.

Thornton slithered up beside T. I. and peered through a thin veil of grass and leaves at the men sitting alongside a narrow, well-used trail. The squad's weapons were neatly stacked in a tepeelike arrangement at the path's center. Thornton acknowledged T. I.'s index finger pointing first up, then down the trail as he indicated where the guards were. If the NVA had put out flank security they'd have been alerted to the SOG team long before. For whatever reasons, they hadn't, much to Thornton's satisfaction. He recognized one of the men as General Vo Liu Dong, supreme commander and

HMFC of the NVA's tactical think tank in Hanoi. What the man was doing here Thornton couldn't imagine, but he was sure it would have to do with the planning of a major operation against either U.S. or South Vietnamese forces.

As Thornton reviewed his study of Dong, he recalled the general's responsibility for three major French disasters while he'd been a battalion commander under Ho himself. Promoted during the transition between French disengagement and United States' entry into Vietnam, Vo Liu Dong left the battlefield to study American tactical doctrine to successfully exploit its weaknesses. His insight into U.S. policy and military application became responsible for more than one Army and Marine field commander's downfall, and MACV had made Dong a priority target for either aerial, naval, or man-initiated assassination.

Obviously Dong had avoided all three, thought Thornton as he watched the lean-hipped general casually stir a small cooking pot of rice while his bodyguards chatted away beside him. Catching T. I.'s mildly amused eye, Thornton indicated the team would engage the squad. The Apache nodded, raising his head a fraction of an inch over Bo's prone figure to pass the unspoken word to the three men now lying on line facing the trail. At that moment Dong himself ordered the point and rear guard to come in. Two of the men nearest the general quickly stuffed small, sticky balls of wet rice into their mouths as they prepared to relieve their comrades.

Bo waited until he was sure all of the men were within his team's waiting sights before signaling the ambush with a white-hot burst of twenty rounds into the smiling face of General Dong. The staff officer's features were instantly obliterated under the high-velocity impact of the 5.56 copper-jacketed hornets, his body thrown backward as the full magazine's contents dumped thousands of pounds of kinetic energy into the man's shattered skull.

The NVA squad reacted as one, throwing themselves down in an attempt to dodge the wall of fire. Donald O'Grady, the team's cherry RTO, without mercy pumped the action of his shotgun into the scramble of bodies not ten feet away. O'Grady had spent some time with the Australian SAS, where he'd learned the value of a scattergun in jungle warfare. Before beginning his second tour, the Special Forces sergeant had picked up a Remington 870, cutting its barrel back and stock down so it was little more than sixteen inches long overall. Slung from his neck and backed up by a .30-caliber M-2 carbine, the system was extremely effective, given the distances SOG normally made contact within. O'Grady preferred to load his own rounds for the shotgun, removing buckshot and replacing it with between twelve to fifteen tightly packed dimes per cartridge. As the coins left the pump gun's barrel they formed a wide pattern of spinning death, opening huge gaps in whatever was unfortunate enough to be in O'Grady's line of sight.

An NVA soldier was caught flush in the belly by the first of O'Grady's expensive canisters, the miniature silver gongs gouging out the PAVN trooper's entrails and dumping them in a heap trailside. Without pause the weapon's terrible snout swept up the right flank of the kill zone, chopping and slicing through uniforms and tan-colored canvas webbing in an orgy of cordite and barely controlled recoil. Emptying the Remington's tube magazine, O'Grady spun the smoking weapon behind him on its sling and began triggering three-round bursts from his M-2. All the while he was screaming at the top of his lungs, although he wouldn't remember doing so afterward.

Thornton's own CAR-15 was well into its third magazine. The heavy *buuuurp* of the two Nung mercenaries weapons jackhammered away on the other side of O'Grady. Whipping the black gun's barrel toward the sliver of a movement from the edge of the jungle opposite him, Thornton hoped as he sent a barrage of nasal decongestants downrange that no one would start heaving hand grenades out of sheer enthusiasm. They weren't but ten feet from the path's well-worn surface, too close to use frags without endangering themselves more than they already were.

Suddenly it was quiet. As if heeding an unspoken cue, the team broke contact, only one of the Nungs chewing through several corpses around the demolished rice pot with well-placed shots on single fire with his AK. Admonished by O'Grady to cease fire, the Nung sheepishly did so, a great grin plastered to his face.

"Jackson," barked Bo while he rammed a fourth magazine into the CAR, "quick-check the bodies while I strip Mr. Moto's map case and ruck from him!"

"Roger that." The Indian slid into the kill zone. In his right hand he held the tomahawk low, its keen edge glinting. Moving from his left, the Apache kicked and tugged at each body, careful not to miss any sign which would reveal a live grenade trapped under a corpse, or a live "corpse" waiting for payback.

Thornton bounded out of his position, the carbine

grasped tightly in his hands as he sidestepped the smoking remains of O'Grady's first casualty. His nostrils flared from the raw smell of freshly let blood. Slipping and nearly falling after stepping heavily on a severed hand lying in the middle of the now-sodden pathway, Bo recovered his balance just as he reached Dong's headless body.

"Hey, Bo, you need a 'hand' out there?" chirped O'Grady from where he still lay with the Nungs.

Asshole, thought Thornton. Still, he couldn't suppress a grin. Slipping his Randall from its well-oiled sheath, Thornton neatly sliced the dead officer's map case from its sling, tossing it back across the trail for O'Grady to stuff into his already-open rucksack. Grabbing a handful of bloody uniform, Bo jerked Dong's body upright, cutting through each shoulder strap so that the general's own canvas ruck fell away with a tiny thump behind him. Nodding his head in satisfaction, Thornton was thankful he'd elected to shoot the NVA officer in the face rather than the body. The well-maintained haversack was undamaged. Tugging the ruck from behind the still-upright corpse, Bo was about to leave the general when he noticed Dong's belt buckle.

Mounted on a carefully oiled and polished brown leather belt was a heavy brass buckle with a pair of French jump wings painstakingly inset into the brass. Thornton had no doubts where Dong had gotten the wings, knowing the general had specialized in destroying French paratroop units. The Sogger once again slipped the double-edged Randall from its sheath, cutting through the thick leather strap on either side of the buckle, then shoving the dead Frenchman's wings into an empty breast pocket on his tigers.

He let the stinking body fall backward, turning to T. I. Jackson just as the Indian reached the last NVA body in the trail. Thornton gasped as the "body" launched itself toward the team's point man, a stubby Russian bayonet clutched in the NVA soldier's blood-covered hand. Before he or the others could issue a warning, Jackson reacted like a snake striking.

Whipping the tomahawk upward, the Indian deftly reversed the ancient weapon so that the long hickory handle was now out front, the heavy hatchet's head upside down, edge outward in his grip. Without a sound, T. I. met the charge, sidestepping, at the same time slapping the NVA soldier hard across his upper back as the man passed. As the startled Vietnamese realized his predicament, he spun on his heels, lunging back toward Jackson, who now held the tomahawk out in front of him at a forty-five-degree angle, edge down.

As the bayonet began to arc upward toward his face, Jackson moved a step to his right, slapping the knife away. The NVA couldn't stop in time to avoid the Apache's snap kick to his unprotected belly, a blow that dropped him to his knees. With a guttural yell of triumph, the Indian slipped behind the collapsed soldier, raising the tomahawk high, then driving it downward with every ounce of energy he could muster. The blade split the NVA's collarbone with an audible snap, proceeding well into the man's chest cavity. Jackson had to place a booted foot against the dead man's back to free the buried blade, the sound of the tomahawk tearing free one that Thornton would never forget.

O'Grady's strained voice unleashed itself as T. I. wiped the bloody blade clean on his pants leg. "Bo! I got a Jolly Green inbound along with a SARTF escort. They can extract within ten mikes if we can reach our primary by then."

Thornton nodded. "Anyone hit?" he asked, hoping against hope the team had come through unscathed. Wounded men were a One-Zero's worst nightmare, given the normally shitty circumstances a team came under fire in. Getting wounded out was both a matter of pride and a challenge. Thornton knew of SOG personnel who had killed themselves before allowing their teams to attempt to extract them. He wasn't sure he had that kind of mettle, and he didn't particularly want to find out.

Burping a sigh of relief that everyone on Python was whole, Bo pointed his CAR's muzzle down the trail, already hearing the rustle and high-pitched voices of the NVA main body as they attempted to locate Dong's encounter with CCN's best guns. "Jackson, you got the point! Cut and run for the PZ but watch your front."

With a nod, the Apache turned and began loping down the trail. One of the Nungs fell in behind him, with O'Grady, with the second mercenary following. Thornton elected to pull the tail gunner's position, jogging several steps at a time, then spinning with his carbine held waist-high as he checked their rear. They'd covered a hundred meters or so when the first NVA scout burst into Thornton's view, to be terminated with a quick burst of ten across the knees. "Go! Go! Go!" screamed the now-kneeling team leader. Thornton pulled a frag from his pistol belt, jerking the pin free and underhanding it up the trail, where it exploded with a weighty *cruuump*!

Not waiting to see what the results might be, the veteran One-Zero turned and began running like a madman down the trail, hearing nothing but his own heart beating inside his chest.

Single shots sounded on either flank of the team as they twisted and turned down the jungle trail. O'Grady fell once, then twice, then a third time, his cursing drifting back over Thornton. Overhead the first Cobra gunship flared into view, Thornton too busy watching the back of the man in front of him to acknowledge the pilot's brisk wave. Suddenly they all burst into a shaded clearing, dropping in exhausted heaps to form a wagon-wheel perimeter from which to fight. "Get commo and get us outta here!" yelled Thornton to his RTO.

O'Grady, his mouth already moving against the handset's black plastic mouthpiece, yanked a yellow smoke grenade from a pouch on his combat harness. Catching one of the Nungs' eyes, the Sogger tossed the canister to the waiting mercenary, who jerked its pin free, rolling the now-burning grenade into the clearing's center.

The sound of the Cobras nosing down around the team's extraction point brought a nervous smile to everyone's face, although Thornton would remember their features stretched tight over the framework of facial bone. Downdraft hit the circle as the CH-53 slipped in above them. On the back ramp they saw an Air Force PJ strapped in behind his GAU-2 minigun, its multiple barrels engaging unseen targets along the trail. Hot extractions were worse than hot LZs, cursed Thornton. You were so close to getting out of another shitty situation, so close to beating the Reaper one more time. Slamming another magazine into his rifle, he squeezed a burst at a flicker of movement.

Within seconds the extraction ladder unrolled itself from the 53's ramp. As the first rung struck the ground, Jackson began clambering upward, clipping himself into the spiderlike framework once he was well above the rest of the team. Both Nungs were next, zipping up behind the Apache without effort, their own snap links securing them in place. A long burst of AK fire roared out of the tree line, catching one of the mercenaries full in the back, killing him instantly. The ladder was moving laterally across the clearing now, O'Grady up and chasing it as the pilot fought to keep his airframe in position despite the intensity of the enemy's ground fire.

Leaping for the aluminum rungs, O'Grady missed the elusive ladder and fell face forward onto the hard-packed jungle floor. Thornton's heart crawled up his throat, beating now so wildly he thought he'd choke. He was in the eye of a maelstrom now, the slapping of the huge chopper's rotors whipping pieces of loose shit around like bits of natural shrapnel. The NVA commander was throwing everything he had against the team, success denied him only because the Cobras were clogging the trail and its flanks with hailstorms of 7.62 lead.

Suddenly the RTO was on his feet again, grabbing the ladder and shooting up it like a red-assed monkey. Thornton didn't wait a moment longer, scrambling along on his hands and knees for the bottom rung, again skipping and jerking around the clearing like a droplet of grease in a frying pan. Reaching the silver stairway, Bo jammed one foot onto the rung, stretching himself to his full height and clipping the safety line up as high as he could reach. He could see the bottom of O'Grady's jungle boots, clogged with mud and bits of flesh from where he'd run through the carnage of the ambush earlier. A steady rain of blood was fanned down over the two Americans, the dead Nung's body hanging loosely, still attached to the extraction ladder.

High above the team, the PJ received a thumbs-up from Thornton, leaning out from the ladder and waving his clenched fist so the gunner could see they were ready to lift out of the rapidly shrinking PZ. With a powerful surge, the Jolly Green began moving forward and up, dragging the string of still-firing recon men behind it as if they were the tail of an oddly shaped kite. Fighting to keep his footing on the bottom rung, Thornton emptied his weapon into the clearing. He forced himself to watch as the ground raced away, gasping as altitude revealed a horde of NVA regulars converging on their microdot of an extraction point. Tiny balls of fire raced after the helicopter. Thornton grabbed the ladder as the pilot threw his ship into an evasive turn, the centrifugal force whipping them out away from the chopper so that it seemed the team was flying along on a magic carpet of chain link and aluminum. "I hate this shit, I hate it, I hate it, I hate it!" yelled the One-Zero as loud as he could.

But deep inside he knew he loved it.

CHAPTER

7

"Sir?"

Thornton opened his eyes as the satin-soft voice of the flight attendant erased the beat of a chopper long since abandoned off the coast of Vietnam. Next to him, Frank was still reading the worn issue of *Time*, his glass empty as was the crumpled bag of airline-issue peanuts handed out soon after they'd taken off.

"Sir, are you going to want a meal this evening?" Unlike many of the stewardesses these days, this one was a looker. A tall gal with a thick mane of long golden hair, the ultimate California surf bunny. The perfectly tailored airline uniform failed to disguise an extremely robust figure, and Thornton noticed she favored a spring-like perfume, which accented her aura of freshness.

"Stop staring and tell the lady what you want." Hartung said, magazine closed now, he caught the girl's eye and smiled widely. "He's never seen a woman before, Miss. The lad was raised by tiny horrible ogres, real mean bastards. You'll have to forgive his shyness."

The stew's laugh was audible sunshine, light with a pleasant, low pitch to it. Thornton squirmed uncomfortably in his seat, caught off guard on all fronts, the sticky wetness of the Nung's air-cooled blood still on his mind. "Eat? No, maybe later, though. Could I get a Black Jack Daniel, lots of ice, straight?"

"One of those for me, too, sweetheart. But I'll be eating," added Frank.

The young woman nodded at both their requests, taking a moment to adjust Thornton's pillow before she moved down the aisle. As she moved past them, Bo felt her squeeze a well-formed hip against his shoulder, and then she was gone. Not bad, he thought to himself with a half smile. Even almost married I've still got the touch. Suddenly he remembered he hadn't spoken with Linda before they'd left San Diego. He'd have to call her from Anchorage to let her know both he and Jason would be out of the net for at least ten days. She'd need to send some personal equipment up for both of them, Thornton's other ballistic knife and at least two extra blades at the top of the list.

"Sleep well?" asked Frank.

"How long have I been out?" countered Bo as the blond returned with their drinks.

"An hour or so."

Taking a timid sip of the strong, cold whiskey, Thornton glanced over to where Bailey and Silver sat, both men's attention centered on a small board between their first-class seats. The JD slid down his throat easily, washing away the sharp tang of recently burned cordite, which lingered in his mind.

"What'd you dream about, 'Nam?"

Startled, Bo turned to face the retired sergeant major whose own drink was already half-empty. "Yeah, how'd you know?"

Frank slid the wide-mouthed plastic glass across the tray in front of him. Hartung's career spanned thirty years of service in uniform. He'd fought in two wars and a half dozen police actions by his own count. He didn't count the hundreds of visits he'd made to countries around the world while wearing the beret, some of them nothing more than well-paid vacations, most with a gun and several full magazines at his side. He'd met Thornton while the two of them were with SOG, and they'd stayed in touch ever since. The dive shop had been the younger man's idea, and Hartung had been more than happy to accept Bo's offer of a partnership as his own retirement crept up on him. The marketplace didn't offer much for a man who could jump out of airplanes, rappel from helicopters, and hit a man dead center at a thousand meters with a $5000 sniper rifle.

Checking the gold Rolex on his wrist, Hartung reminded himself they'd done pretty well on the outside. Heavy Hook was thriving, thanks to some savvy business moves and a good location. San Diego was growing, the overspill from Los Angeles forcing people southward toward the border. The Navy's special ops community was likewise expanding with three SEAL teams now out at Coronado along with the SpecWar Center and its attendant courses. With the additional income provided by Springblade's last three missions for the government, he and Thornton had been able to expand the shop's spectrum of classes to include individual swimmer delivery systems and underwater photography. With Bo living up in Oregon these days, Frank pretty much ran the business alone, which was fine with both men.

"Well, how'd you know I was dreaming about the war? Was I grinding my teeth or what?"

Draining his glass before answering, Hartung caught the pretty stew's eye once more, indicating he'd like coffee with his meal. "You started whispering in your sleep. The only time you do that is when you're back in 'Nam. Which mission?"

Bo grunted. Whispering in his sleep! When he'd left after his last tour with SOG it had taken him nearly three months to learn how to speak English again, his language pattern a mixture of Vietnamese, Chinese, and half a dozen other dialects he'd picked up after spending months at a time in the bush. They'd salted him away at Bragg, finding him a job with the Special Warfare Center until he'd shaken three tours free. "Dong, General Vo Liu Dong. I blew him away again."

Hartung nodded. "That was a damn fine job. Dong was an architect, a professional war maker. If I remember correctly, MACV was able to pinpoint three major NVA command complexes with what you brought back. Not to mention the operations the grunts mounted against the area you came out of."

"You ever dream about Vietnam, Frank?"

At that moment the blond reappeared with their food. Within seconds she'd served them, filling Hartung's cup with coffee as well as Thornton's. In a moment she was gone, her fragrance lingering until the overhead air jets above the two men blew it away.

Slicing into the steak in front of him, Frank Hartung

chewed silently for a moment before answering. Outside the huge airliner it was dark, the ground 36,000 feet below invisible. Hartung enjoyed flying, it was the next thing on his list he wanted to learn how to do. "Nope," he finally said. "I never dream about Vietnam, Bo. Not that you shouldn't. Hell, that's about as normal a thing as I can imagine. Anyone who's been to war dreams about it at one time or another.

"I don't dream about the 'Nam because it didn't show me nothing I hadn't seen before. By the time Sergeant Franklin Hartung was introduced to the war, he'd seen the bear and knew the devil's secret name and face. Remember, Bo, I was in Korea. *That* was a war, my friend.

"In Korea we damn near got our asses kicked before knowing we even had an ass! Our equipment was World War Two vintage, our officers mostly snot-nosed kids who never believed they'd have to lead men into combat. The terrain was every bit as shitty as Vietnam, but it was the weather that smoked you like a cheap cigar. Hot as hell's own afterburners in the summer, and cold as an ex-wife's heart during winter. I watched my friends freeze to death, lose limbs to frostbite, go crazy after days of seeing nothing but white. Vietnam was a paradise after Korea, a sheer paradise.

"Worse than all that shit was the enemy, though. In Vietnam we fought against shadows mostly. Sure, the NVA changed all that once they started rolling south, but you find me a grunt from the Twenty-fifth or the Ninth who saw more than maybe fifty or sixty live dinks in the course of his tour. Now, you and I ran into shitloads of the bastards, but only because we were silly enough to go sneaking around in the Man's backyard, where he didn't expect us.

"But in Korea, Bo, in Korea they came at us in waves. More than once I knew I was a dead man watching literally thousands of the mothers storming across the frozen snow, their bayonets glinting in the sun or shining under our parachute flares. God, they were insane in their desire to kill us. We'd burn the barrels out of machine guns, then go hand to hand until one side or the other broke.

"So I don't dream about Vietnam like you do, son. When I start whispering in my sleep it's because I hear bugles and see ten thousand motherfuckers lining up just out of range. My dreams begin and end in a war this country didn't forget because it never remembered it took place to begin with. My nightmares, if that's what you want to call them, are of Korea."

Both men finished their meals in silence. The stew slipped their trays out from in front of them, aware the two were somehow more than just traveling companions or friends. She noticed both were wearing similar gold rings, each bearing the same military crest on its face. They and the two sitting across from them weren't her regular fare of airline passenger. She liked the younger man whose arm she'd graced with a subtle bump of her generous rear end, but he'd shown her no more than polite attention ever since.

Returning with an after-dinner menu of pastries and drinks, she was surprised to find both men fast asleep.

CHAPTER

8

Chuikov sat back in his chair and surveyed the equipment he'd carefully laid out across the king-size bed of his hotel room. The American company had done well, delivering all he'd ordered within twenty-four hours. What marvelous efficiency, he thought to himself. It would have taken twenty-four days in Russia . . . and even then half of what was ordered wouldn't arrive. Grabbing a yellow legal pad from the floor, Chuikov began checking items off the short list it possessed. When finished, he realized he was missing some minor foodstuffs as well as a knife. Both the shotgun and rifle were already loaded, the Beretta slipped comfortably inside the waistband of his Levis. He needed to make one more shopping trip, then contact the pilot who had agreed to fly him inland that afternoon.

Shrugging into a light summer jacket that covered the 9-mm's bulky grip, the Spetsnaz commando quickly arranged several items in his room that, if found disturbed, would alert him to the fact he'd been discovered. Slipping into the hallway, he checked his door to make sure it was locked, then casually entered the stairwell just one door down from his own. In minutes he was out on the street, heading toward the downtown area.

Fairbanks, Alaska, is the last of the good-time cities. A jumping-off point for gold miners and trappers during the state's heyday as "the final frontier," the legends and ghosts of this charming town include actual personalities such as Jack London, the writer, and Dangerous Dan McGrew, a fictional gunfighter and gambler made famous in doggerel. Fairbanks hasn't changed all that much over the years. The Gold Rush gave way to the Oil Rush in the mid-seventies, and the city grew by leaps and bounds. Its occupants are a sturdy lot, enjoying summers where the temperature reaches 100 degrees F during peak months and braving winters which drop to 70 below on a good day. There still exist trappers and mountain men who venture into town once every half year to replenish their supply sacks and sell furs. Being armed is a way of life this far north, gun control being a matter of hitting what you're shooting at.

Chuikov was ignored as he made his way toward the Northern Commercial Company store off Second Street. He could have been a mining expert, a logger, or one of the professors from the college above Farmer's Loop for all anyone knew or cared. It was a wonderful anonymity for the hard-bitten soldier, a freedom he was unused to, yet immediately comfortable with. Wandering down aisles flanked with goods, the Russian was reminded of how poorly his countrymen were taken care of by their government. There was no shortage of guns, he thought grimly. No shortage of tanks and planes and poison gases with which to lay waste to those outside the communist sphere of influence. In America there was no shortage of possibility; in Russia possibility had to do more with an individual's arrest than achievement.

Reaching the sporting-goods section, the Soviet colonel was drawn to a long display counter by the building's far wall. Inside under glass were rows upon rows of both custom and production blade ware. Chuikov directed the eager young man behind the counter to a red-scaled folder known as a Swiss Army knife, one of the most practical edged tools an outdoorsman or soldier could carry. Taking his time, Chuikov examined the long-bladed sheath knives before him. The Russian had grown up with knives and hatchets, and he knew them well. Finally he chose a massive Moran-inspired Rio Grande bowie. The blade had a ten-inch carbon-steel blade with a stout point and slight clip grind along the top of the blade. The razorlike belly reached forward from the brass double guard all the way to the broad tip in a subtle curve that featured a hard-hitting rolled edge for superior chopping and cutting. Chuikov hefted the big knife, its contoured Rosewood slabs slipping into his hand as if it had been made specifically for him. "This one, too," he told the smiling clerk.

A few minutes later he was back on the crowded streets of Fairbanks with a sack full of freeze-dried foods in one arm, the two knives already tucked away where they couldn't be seen on his person. Chuikov knew the power that came from the barrel of a gun, but he also knew the fear that was fanned at the sight of a truly big knife. Let the wolves come, he told himself. Let them come and taste their own blood!

Ducking into the darkened Cheena Bar, Chuikov dropped a quarter into the pay phone just inside the entrance. He was only half-aware of the curious stares directed at him by the bar's occupants, all of whom were Eskimo. Dialing Foster's number at SOCOM by memory, he waited until the recorder left for him was activated before feeding the drop coordinates for the recovery team into the phone's mouthpiece. Hanging up, he turned to leave, bumping into a burly Indian who now blocked his exit. With a smile Chuikov spoke rapidly in the man's native tongue, brushing past the Indian as he did so.

Out on the street again, Chuikov laughed to himself at the surprise on the drunk's face. White men for the most part knew little to nothing about Alaska's native tribes. On the other hand, Spetsnaz units assigned missions inside the forty-ninth state knew *everything* about the land's resources, which included its original settlers. Chuikov himself spoke several dialects, and he knew of at least three other Spetsnaz commandos who spoke more. Being able to communicate with those with or against whom they were working was a mandatory skill within Soviet special operations.

As Chuikov crossed the busy main avenue in front of the ancient post office he reminded himself of just how misinformed the Americans were about Spetsnaz. Often associated with the KGB, Spetsnaz was in fact under the command of the GRU, or Soviet military intelligence. With a total strength of about 30,000 troops, not to mention another 150,000 reservists with Spetsnaz active-duty experience, Russia possessed the largest body of special-forces operatives in the world. Almost all its members were drawn from the rolls of the Young Communist League or Voluntary Society for Cooperation with the Army, Air Force, and Fleets. Spetsnaz troopers served with either the army or the navy, a blue or black beret their distinctive headgear.

Unlike the American Green Berets, whose mission was a sophisticated blend of covert, overt, and overseas drill-sergeant duties, Spetsnaz forces were direct action in nature with no thought given to winning either hearts or minds. Chuikov's troops were targeted toward specific political and material objectives. They were diversionary and destruction orientated, dedicated to mission accomplishment no matter the environment or odds. The Spetsnaz elite like Chuikov were utilized in sensitive political situations where discussion was unnecessary because a bullet, bomb, or knife ended the debate. The microchips that were elaborately hidden away in Colonel Chuikov's newly purchased rucksack held the entire GRU order of battle for Spetsnaz deployment into Alaska. Targets included key local and federal government officials, military installations and personnel, lines of communication, and vital resource centers. Chuikov possessed the key to the Russian assault on Alaska should the two superpowers ever go to war, a key he was betting would open the door to freedom for him.

Checking his watch, the Russian noted silently he had less than an hour left before meeting his pilot. Snagging the receiver of yet another pay phone, he contacted the man, giving the name of the hotel he was staying in as well as a time for them to meet. Because it was summer, Chuikov didn't have to worry about how late he landed in the area chosen for his wilderness sanctuary. The ''Land of the Midnight Sun'' wouldn't see darkness until well past midnight, giving him more than enough time to move several klicks before stringing a bivi-tent and getting some sleep.

Satisfied that all was well at the pilot's end, Chuikov slipped once again into the mainstream traffic of Fairbanks. Moving at a brisk pace toward his hotel, he arrived within five minutes, this time taking the elevator back to his room. Inside, he checked each of the passive traps laid before leaving, pleased they remained undisturbed. Shrugging out of the lightweight jacket that concealed his weaponry, the Spetsnaz commando slipped his newly purchased items into the spacious pockets of his ruck, leaving the thick-bladed Rio Grande out so that he could carry it on his belt. Hefting the shotgun, he strapped it to the outside of the pack, carefully adjusting the rack of six 12-gauge rounds mounted off the receiver's left side. Loading the M-77 with five high-velocity rounds of .223 madness, Chuikov moved to the single window facing the street and adjusted the rifle's scope. Standing well back from the glass so that he couldn't be observed from below, the professional sniper whisked the cross hairs across a dozen unsuspecting citizens, mentally calculating angles and distance as he selected a mark before squeezing an imaginary trigger.

Some old habits die hard, he mused before putting the rifle away.

CHAPTER 9

"The man says he left yesterday, taking the train to Fairbanks, where he made arrangements for a room. Fortunately for us, the colonel continues to use his credit card to make reservations. Without it we might have lost him." Yuri Pushkin finished his sentence by dropping into one of the hard-bottomed chairs pulled out from the small kitchen of their safe house. His team's infiltration into Alaska had gone unnoticed by American security forces, a textbook exercise. Once safely ashore, they'd been met by a parallel agent to the one used by Chuikov. It was then that Pushkin learned her counterpart had been detained for questioning, although he was currently free and around town. Climbing aboard an expensive motor home containing a previously cached supply of weapons, clothing, and forged documents, the Spetsnaz team had traveled in style to Anchorage, where they'd been met by the agent who'd spotted Chuikov earlier. The safe house he'd prepared was actually north of the city in a town called Eagle River. It was tucked away near a small river, isolated from its neighbors and ignored by delivery vehicles.

"Why use the card, Yuri? The colonel knows it can be traced almost as soon as the number is entered into the computer; it makes no sense." Sergeant Antonov ended his question by tearing a huge bite from the roast beef sandwich in his hand. Dressed in Levis, thick woodsman's boots, and a tight-fitting navy blue pullover, he looked every inch the perfect Alaskan.

Pushkin levered a sandwich of his own from the plateful prepared for them by the woman. "With a credit card he can make his arrangements by phone, such as was done with the equipment flown in from Georgia. Chuikov knows as well as we that he is leaving a trail, but our colonel is counting on a brisk pace to outdistance us."

"Where will he go from Fairbanks, Major?" The speaker was one of the new men provided at Pushkin's request from their sister Spetsnaz team at Ryazan. He was a demolitions expert as well as a superb tracker, with experience in both Afghanistan and Iran, where he had been involved in chasing renegade Kurds.

Pushkin was famished. The long trip without rest from their last mission had left him hungry and tired. Tearing into the sandwich, he devoured half of it before answering the waiting soldier's question. "The bush. Chuikov will find himself a pilot and fly to a remote area where he can operate on the ground. His file shows him to be leery of working in an urban environment, although he is an excellent technician. GRU assessments are that the Americans will respond to the bait offered them by

Chuikov, but not until the colonel has already left for the backcountry."

Antonov rammed a full magazine into the well of his Sig-Sauer P226, the 9-mm automatic's slide snapping a round off the top and chambering it as he hit the slide release with a practiced thumb. "Do we know the Americans are buying what this loathsome traitor has to sell? If so, who should we expect to meet once we've 'convinced' our pilot friend to take us to Chuikov?"

Slipping his own pistol free, this one a Sig P220, which chambered the .45-caliber round Pushkin liked instead of the 9-mm favored by his sergeant, the Spetsnaz major racked the slide back and inserted a fresh magazine from the stack at his feet. The team's weapons had all been purchased over a period of time from stores scattered throughout the territory. The rifles were civilian versions of the military M-16, each having received a few adjustments so they now had full-auto selector switches. In addition to a rifle and twenty-five magazines, each Spetsnaz commando carried either a P220 or P226 from Sig-Sauer, along with five extra magazines. There were four American fragmentation grenades per trooper, as well as six claymore antipersonnel mines for the team's nighttime security. Each was issued a Gerber-made hatchet as well as an MK II fighting knife, although Pushkin knew Antonov was carrying a Spetsnaz-issue ballistic knife as well.

"Our sources in Moscow have traced calls coming from the colonel's hotel in Anchorage to a number at Fort Bragg, North Carolina. The first number is assigned to a Special Forces officer whose name is unimportant. Some time ago their paths crossed and Chuikov has chosen this man to be his conduit to political asylum.

"A second number is now being used, but it is both monitored and scrambled; we dare not attempt a tap or we alert the Americans as to how close we are to Chuikov already. This number has been contacted from a phone in the Fairbanks area, although the call did not originate from the hotel room that we have traced through the credit card to Colonel Chuikov.

"To answer your question I believe the Americans will send a selected team of their Green Berets or SEALs to retrieve the colonel from his woodland hideaway. Our best chance of securing the colonel and his information is to allow him to leave Fairbanks, then to search for him on the ground. We know he has at least one beacon with him, and we will use its signal to help guide us to wherever he may decide to await the Americans."

"I can find him without a signal, Comrade Major. No man walks the face of the earth without leaving signs of his passing." The speaker, their new tracker, fixed Pushkin with an icy stare as he slipped the long-bladed Gerber from its black sheath.

"No one doubts your ability to do just that, comrade. In fact, I personally believe it will be your skill that will bring us success long before Chuikov activates his stolen beacon. At the same time we must consider all the possibilities that can affect a mission such as this. Let us not forget we chase one of our own, a man who indeed 'wrote the book,' as our hosts say. We will exercise all of our options to effect the man's capture; it is the only way we will win this race."

Everyone's eyes looked to the door as the woman entered, her short black hair tucked up underneath a dirty woolen cap despite the summer's heat. "Your bird has flown the coop as of an hour ago. Charlie told me to tell you he thinks he knows who the bush pilot is, but we've got to get our asses in gear if we're going to get to Fairbanks before dark."

Without a word the team arose as one, grabbing their prepacked rucksacks and shouldering them as if they weighed but a few pounds. Pistols and knives tucked away from view, they trooped out of the house and toward the waiting Beaver coach. It was a three-hour drive to Fairbanks, Pushkin reminded himself, three hours during which they'd better get what sleep they could before the business of catching the wolf became more than just a chase.

CHAPTER 10

Chuikov watched the plane disappear over the ridge, its wings rocking back and forth in silent farewell as the pilot gracefully lifted the single-engine aircraft over the forest. The sound of the engine came to the Russian, atop his well-provisioned rucksack. The Russian continued sitting alongside the grassy strip of earth where the pilot had touched down. Now all he heard was the sound of the wind chasing itself through the trees around his tiny perimeter. Bird and insects voices combined in harmony with the rustle of huge pine needles and broad-faced leaves. Chuikov felt the sun warming his shoulders and broad back. He'd have to strip to his T-shirt to remain comfortable once he began his trek inland. Already small beads of sweat covered his brow.

Peter Chuikov was as at home in the woods as most men were in their own living rooms. Where the utter isolation of the deep forests might cause panic and depression in some, Chuikov loved solitude. He'd grown up hiking and climbing the mountains of his homeland, taking those early experiences and skills with him into the army.

But this was not Afghanistan, where every crevice might contain a flint-eyed guerrilla hell-bent on cutting Chuikov's nuts off with his long-bladed knife. It wasn't the desolation of Chad, a land left to vaporize under an unforgiving sun. As Chuikov took in his surroundings, he realized he'd never been in such a beautiful place, a place where silence was so complete it screamed. I am at peace, he thought. Overhead an eagle soared, wings stretched wide to catch the currents that carried him aloft.

Adjusting his time-worn patrol cap, one of the few things he'd brought across with him, Chuikov rose. Turning and bending forward, he grabbed the dark blue cordura rucksack by both shoulder straps, heaving it upward and over his head so it sat squarely on his back. Again reaching down, he snagged the black nylon sling of the hunting rifle, hefting its weight upward, grasping the weapon so it rode easily in both hands. The shotgun was strapped securely to the side of the ruck, a round in the chamber and safety engaged. Around his waist the Russian wore a heavy brown belt of saddle leather from which the Rio Grande bowie hung in its black leather sheath. The Beretta was strapped to the opposite side of the belt in a sturdy holster with a top flap, a magazine carrier with two extra clips snuggled in behind it.

The colonel wore a long-sleeved shirt of aqua blue flannel, which he would remove as he began sweating from the exertion he knew was coming. Underneath his black T-shirt he wore a small Finnish utility knife hanging from a leather thong secured around his neck. His Levis were new although washed several times to soften the stiff cotton; a smaller belt of tan canvas bearing Chuikov's Spetsnaz belt buckle encircled his trim waist. The Russian had discarded his heavy boondockers for a pair of modified American jungle boots. Their standard cleated soles had been replaced with a plateless soft tread pattern which made little noise on hard surfaces, and left an almost faceless track in the earth. The boots were considerably lighter than those Chuikov had at first considered, and they would dry quickly should he have to cross water along his route.

Along with his basic camp items, food, and ammunition, the Russian carried a camouflage Gortex jacket for protection against the wind and rain, as well as a black fisherman's sweater he'd bought on impulse in Valdez. There was an extra change of clothes as well as a first-aid kit tucked away at the bottom of the ruck should he need such items. Enough for the comforts of home, he mused aloud. The beacon that would bring the Special Forces team to him was secured in its impact-resistant box, with a spare set of AA batteries. The transmitter was no larger than two packs of playing cards taped together, and it had a range of twenty kilometers in all directions. Chuikov had packed the radio device in one of the outside pockets of his ruck, where he could get to it in a hurry if necessary.

If worse comes to worse I'll simply walk out, he told himself. He had timed his defection to allow him plenty of good weather should the Americans deny him asylum, weather which would give him the best possible odds to trek across the state's vastness and into Canada. He'd taken the precaution of salting away a sterile passport and a good amount of money during an athletic event several Spetsnaz officers had attended as competitors, easily losing his KGB tails as he'd wandered the city pretending to be a tourist. One thing was certain as he broke out a Silva compass and took a quick reading against the memorized map in his mind, Colonel Peter Chuikov, Spetsnaz officer and stalker of men, was dead. In his place a new man had arisen, a man who wanted control over his own destiny and choices in life. It was this man who now stood alone under a brilliant Alaskan sun, and it was this man whom Chuikov was committed to saving at all costs.

Slapping the bolt of his M-77 home, he chambered a round, then began moving at a steady pace toward the gently swaying trees.

CHAPTER 11

The ride from Anchorage International was a quick one. An agent from the local DEA office met the team at the airport and escorted them to their two rental cars. Bailey had spent several minutes with the man exchanging information, nodding curtly at whatever it was the Alaskan drug buster said. Finally both men shook hands, their nameless host walking briskly across the parking lot to a waiting Plymouth.

"Well, what's the scoop?" asked Thornton as Hartung and Silver jumped into the second vehicle, Jason driving. Bailey, adjusting the S&W so that it rode a little higher under his jacket, turned the ignition over as Bo belted himself in on the passenger side. With a small hand signal Calvin bulled his way into the terminal's traffic pattern, Silver close behind as they edged out toward the crowded exit.

"Billings sends his regards. Apparently the State Department as well as NSA have confirmed the value of what Chuikov brought out with him, and the mission's a go. Mike Bannion will be joining us by nightfall—they're flying him in from Korea. With Lee still out of commission I figured we could use an extra hand."

Bo nodded agreement. Bannion, a SLAM agent whose job it was to interdict drug-smuggling routes in Southeast Asia, had joined Springblade as a pinch hitter when the team was sent to San Francisco to protect a Central American political figure. Thornton remembered Bannion well, a former Navy SEAL whose quick thinking had saved them all from a fiery death planned by Major Luis Melendez. Thornton had killed the major that night, impaling the man's heart with the ballistic. "The boys will be happy to have Mike back on board. You staying for the party?"

Grabbing his parking receipt, Bailey deftly tossed it into the car's backseat and headed toward downtown Anchorage. He ordered a suite of rooms for the team, all interconnected so that they could move back and forth freely. Time wise, Springblade would be in the city for less than twenty-four hours; their C–7A Caribou was already being prepared for LALO drop by the pararescue team at Elmendorf Air Force Base. "Yeah, I'll be going in with you even though Billings isn't real happy about it. I told him we needed five people on the ground, especially if there's a Spetsnaz team with the same thought in mind as we've got. Conrad's not real up on his Russian special forces doctrine, but I convinced him they weren't your average GI Joe fantasy figures."

Thornton grinned, looking back over his shoulder to check on Hartung and Silver's progress as they hurried after Bailey. "Any rumblings from the head shed about what the Soviets are doing about all this? If there's a response en route it'd be nice to know about it before we get on the ground."

Settling onto a long straightaway, Bailey jerked a Marlboro from its pack and lit up. "No one's heard anything. Damned GRU is so big that they could hold a hundred meetings and we'd only hear about the ones Moscow wanted us to know about, anyhow. Spetsnaz personnel are impossible to track. Shit, they've got over a hundred thousand of the bastards.

"We did get one interesting tidbit of information out of the Company, but we'd have to confirm its importance with Chuikov himself for it to help much."

"Don't keep me in suspense, squid," intoned Thornton, cracking his window to let some of the lung-choking smoke from Calvin's cigarette escape the car.

Thornton had quit smoking some time ago and never missed the opportunity to remind Calvin of the fact whenever the DEA agent insisted on lighting up. After the two exchanged murderous glances, Calvin continued. "Seems a journalist—one of these combat-photo bums who write for the guns-and-guts crowd—got his head sent into orbit while humping the trails with a band of Afghan freedom fighters . . ."

"Yeah, I saw something on the tube about that the other day. So what else is new? You go looking for trouble and you normally find it, especially in that particular country," interrupted Thornton.

". . . so anyhow, pardon your rudeness, some geeky analyst deep within the bowels of the CI-fucking-A draws a parallel between the method used to kill the writer and some other assassinations that have taken place over the last several years.''

Now interested, Thornton looked over at Bailey, happily puffing away. ''You're saying this poor slob was *assassinated* by someone, not just blown away because he couldn't get the light right for the folks back home?''

''I ain't saying shit, Bo. The agency's intel-geek is doing all the talking, and what he says is that there's been a rash of long-range shootings where the victims' heads turn into sputniks as soon as a particular round blows through their owner's anatomies. The geek says it's a very precise shot that's popping noggins lately, delivered from a seven-point-six-two NATO gun. Word is that Spetsnaz personnel have such a system available, but on a limited basis and only to an elite group of shooters.''

Thornton snorted. ''Doesn't mean shit. Where's the link between Spetsnaz, this journalist, and Chuikov? So some dude gets his rocks off popping heads. Give me a connection and I'll be impressed.''

Hitting his turn signal, Bailey swung the car onto Anchorage's main drag. Ahead they could see the Captain Cook Hotel, where they'd be staying. ''Here's your connection, wise guy. After the journalist got wasted there was a firefight between the shooter and his people and the freedom fighters. The bad guys got away, but not before they'd lost one of their dudes. Our shooter has a few grenades tucked underneath the body as a going-away present, but the Afs have seen this trick before and disarm the body before checking it out.

''What they find is a white man wearing standard-issue Spetsnaz stuff. On top of that, he's got a tiny gold medallion around his throat with a wolf's head engraved in its center.

"The boys know certain other white folk are paying big bucks for this kind of find, so they tote Ivan's dead ass back to a ville, where an Agency field rep fingerprints and photos the corpse. Thank God for computers, because our data geek matches the dead man with a known Spetsnaz operative who attended the Olympics as a contestant a game or two ago. Along with him was another Russian by the name of Yuri Pushkin, who just happens to be suspected of having serious Spetsnaz connections himself—"

"And he's a shooter. I've heard the name mentioned by some of the guys who travel the circuit. Pushkin's supposed to be one of the ultimate scope-and-trigger men on the scene today."

Reaching the hotel, Bailey parked the rental out front, watching in his rearview as Silver tucked the second car up behind them. "Soviet radio traffic for that period contained an urgent request to extract a team of some sort from an LZ near where the ambush took place. Sources in Kabul reported a nonscheduled takeoff from the Russian air base of a Soviet fighter with two personnel on board, destination Moscow. It could be that this Pushkin and his team have been selected to renovate Chuikov's brain-housing group, and if so they *could* already be in country looking for him."

Stepping out of the car, Thornton turned a wary eye toward the young narc. "Is our security up here so shitty that these guys can waltz in and out as they please? First Chuikov blows in like a tourist on vacation, now you're telling me an entire Spetsnaz hit team might be staying in the same hotel as we are? Is there something wrong with this picture, or am I just all fucked up?''

''I'd vote for the latter,'' grumbled Hartung, walking up alongside the fuming commando leader. ''That's the last time I let Silver follow anyone with me in the car,'' he continued. ''The man's incapable of maintaining a tail without endangering everyone on the road around him, or in the car with him. Next time I'll drive.''

Behind them Silver pulled their meager luggage from the trunk, oblivious to his companion's complaints about his lack of road manners. ''Let's get inside and get settled,'' ordered Bo. ''I want everyone to shower and get changed. We'll order food in, and I need the PJs or whoever's got our firepower and personal gear to get it here so we can sort through it.

''At the same time Calvin will need to make sure Mad Mike gets here as soon as possible after he's landed. Frank's in charge of inspecting the plane for tomorrow's jump, Silver will need whatever connections with SO-COM or any other assets we've got available so he can prepare an S-2 briefing later on tonight.''

''No sweat, Bo. I ordered our gear pulled from what the SEALs had available at Coronado before we left. Colt Commandos, the new LBE rigs, Glock 17s with plus-two mags, uniforms, boots, Gortex, the whole shot. You all had your personal shit with you anyhow, so I didn't worry about knives and stuff like that. All I need to do is make a call and the guy we met at the airport will have the stuff brought over from the office.''

Thornton slapped the agent heartily on the back, a broad grin on his face. ''That's great! Frank? Can you get right out to the base and precheck the Caribou? The

PJs are the best in the business but I want to know we've got everything we need in place for a LALO.''

''Airborne and amen,'' barked the veteran paratrooper. ''We going out at two-fifty?'' he asked.

''Roger that,'' replied Bo. ''SOCOM says Chuikov will be using a beacon and is supposed to have passed grid coordinates for our DZ before going to ground. We'll pop at two-fifty, be in the air for less than twenty seconds, then rally up and listen for the colonel's beacon signal.''

''Sounds like a piece of cake to me,'' exclaimed Silver who'd just joined the group.

''I sure as hell hope you're right, Jason. If we've got a team from the other side working the same AO, our smart-assed plan could go to hell in a handbasket. Chuikov's going to leave a trail no matter how hard he tries not to. If Pushkin's been elected to bring the colonel's head back to Red Square, you know he'll have every bit of support the GRU can muster, and they don't have to play by anyone's rules but their own.''

Bailey nodded, tapping Thornton gently on the shoulder. ''With that in mind let's get our asses inside, eh? I don't like the idea of hanging around out here too long, especially if what you say is true. No doubt the Soviets have a network of agents active, and they might be staking out likely spots for Chuikov to show up at.''

The men grabbed their belongings and entered the hotel.

CHAPTER 12

The drive from Eagle River to Fairbanks had taken them no time at all, the road as clear as the weather. The man known only to Pushkin as "Charlie" was part of the two-man cell that had originally recognized Colonel Chuikov at the mall. Charlie's common-law wife knew nothing of her husband's political leanings, believing him to be involved as he had been for years in illegal drug and gun smuggling. In the rear of the big motor home Pushkin was relaxing as the others slept. Their guide was certain he knew who had flown Chuikov into the bush; a few phone calls and some cash had turned up that bit of information. The Spetsnaz major wasn't concerned with how they'd convince the pilot to repeat his earlier flight, Sergeant Major Antonov would see to that. He was concerned, however, with what the Americans might be doing. Pushkin had had no contact whatsoever with Vasili Suworov after leaving the marshal's office in Moscow. Every portal the Spetsnaz team passed through was closed and sealed behind them, a precaution against direct Russian involvement becoming public knowledge should Pushkin's team fail. It was a classic total-enclosure mission; like strategic recon, either everybody or nobody was coming out alive once it was all over.

"We're here," barked Charlie as he manhandled the huge rig onto a short drive leading up to a small hangar. Pushkin swung his legs off the bed he was occupying, seeing Antonov's figure already moving to the front of the Beaver. Slipping his Gerber from where he'd laid it earlier, Pushkin shoved the black sheath down behind his belt, pulling the lower lip of his sweater down over the shadow black handle. Motioning to the others to stay where they were, the Russian clambered up behind the driver, squinting through the bug-covered windshield at the open hangar door.

"My squeal told me our boy here made a special flight just yesterday. Flew a single soul into the backcountry and got paid cash on delivery. Supposed to fly a return leg in about ten days to check on the client—"

"Who won't be there," finished Pushkin. Turning to Antonov, he pointed at the figure of a man who'd wandered out from the gloom of the hangar's interior to watch the lumbering motor home lurch to a stop. "Make contact, confirm the man's identity, and convince him we will pay him for his services by allowing him to live. Do not damage his hands, feet, or face. Remember, he is a pilot and we need his skill and memory to take us to Chuikov."

Antonov smiled. "Not to worry, Comrade Major." With that the agile noncom opened the passenger door of the mobile home and dropped to the tarmac below him. Both Charlie and Pushkin watched as Antonov engaged the pilot in conversation, each involuntarily jerking as the Russian suddenly grabbed the man by the front of his shirt and swept the pilot's legs out from beneath him with one well-executed kick. Antonov followed his initial attack with a mighty blow to the man's belly with his knee, a move that caved the unfortunate punching bag's middle in, dropping his head to the tire-marked concrete runway. Stepping behind the heaving figure, Antonov grabbed hold of the pilot's ankles and spread his legs wide apart. Lifting the struggling figure a foot off the ground, the Russian unloaded a steel-toed boot between the man's legs, dropping him as a fresh spurt of vomit exploded from the now-crying man's mouth. By now the entire team, including Charlie's grinning wife, were bunched up in the driver's compartment, their rapt attention pinioned to the scene taking place before them.

Pushkin waited as Antonov knelt beside the pilot, obviously talking with the man who writhed in pain. With a triumphant smile Antonov looked up, his thumb in the air as he gesticulated the success of his hands-on interrogation. "Let's go!" growled Pushkin. "We've no time to waste. Antonov will determine what plane we'll need to take while I meet with the pilot and attempt to soothe his battered ego."

Turning to the man called Charlie, Pushkin pointed to where he had been lying moments before. "Under the bed you will find your reward. The marshal will be highly pleased with your service; I myself will inform him upon my return. After we have left, you may return to Anchorage. I suggest you carry on as if you'd never made this trip. No one will be the wiser and we will not be returning."

Charlie nodded. His wife slipped into the driver's chair as her husband began helping Pushkin's team unload their gear. Antonov had pulled the whimpering pilot to his knees as Pushkin approached the two men, his Gerber pressed lightly against the wildly pumping artery now clearly visible in the man's throat. "You will fly us to where you dropped Chuikov, yes?" he asked.

"Don't, don't know no man named Cheweecough," wheezed the pilot. "Took a big fella out yesterday, though. . . . Name was Chandler; don't know no Cheweecough, though," gasped the injured flier.

"Chandler will do nicely," comforted Pushkin. "We need a plane large enough to transport five men and their equipment. Is there such an aircraft available?"

The pilot nodded weakly, feeling the lean cutting edge whispering around his throat even as he spoke. "I got two birds of my own. One's just for single parties, two passengers at the most, plus gear. The other fits your bill—two-engine turbo parked behind the hangar. She's gassed and ready, just got to fire up the engines."

Dropping to one knee, the Spetsnaz commando looked directly into the wounded pilot's fear-glazed eyes. His voice was low, the words spoken with the measured cadence of a man who is so sure of himself that he has no need to do more than transmit his desires in the most civilized manner possible, knowing they'll be carried out immediately if not sooner. "Take us to him and you will return with not only your life, but ten thousand dollars to boot. Fail, and I will let this man finish his work."

The pilot paled under Pushkin's threat. Pulled to his

feet by Antonov, he gestured toward where the larger plane was sitting. "I'll fly you, mister. Anywhere, anytime, any price you're willing to pay. If you got business with Mr. Chandler it ain't mine to know about. Just let me go afterward and you can keep the money. All I want is my ass in one piece."

Fifteen minutes later they were airborne.

CHAPTER 13

Calvin Bailey sauntered from the bathroom, his muscular torso swathed in a thick white towel. Rubbing his scalp briskly, he watched as Thornton finished cleaning his new Glock, courtesy of SEAL Team 3. The Glock was one of the newest pieces in the Navy special warfare inventory, a 9-mm handgun whose frame consisted of a space-age polymer that was tougher and lighter than most conventional automatics. Bailey had opted for the standard Glock 17, although the smaller Model 19 had been offered. Along with the weapons, he'd gotten the rugged polymer holsters and magazine holders made specifically for the gun. Using plus-two magazines, each man would be carrying fifty-seven rounds of subsonic ammunition around his waist with a weight factor of half any other high-capacity 9-mm auto-loader. The narc himself was taking one of the weapons in, leaving his trusted S&W behind. "How's it look?" he asked as Thornton slipped the steel slide onto the frame's runners.

Taking a moment to brusquely thrust a full magazine up the Glock 17's well, Thornton gently squeezed the unique trigger system until he felt the firing pin pop forward. Racking the slide so it picked up a round, he chambered the 9-mm hollow-point by allowing the upper receiver to fly forward under its own spring-driven power. Satisfied with his work, the spec-war specialist tossed the pistol onto his bed, then turned to Bailey, who was beginning to dress. "Good weapon. We musta fired over five thousand rounds apiece on San Clemente with them. Gotta admit I'm tempted to go back to a "nine" now that I've worked with Dr. Glock, though my P220 is a hard mother to beat when it comes to close-in work."

Bailey tugged a pair of Levis up around his waist, belting them into place and slipping his own Glock into its low-profile holster at his side. "Not to change the subject, but I need to crank up the scrambler and give Billings a call. He's our POC with this Colonel Foster at SOCOM, and I need to confirm the coordinates for our drop so Frank can get us squared away."

With a nod, Thornton reached into his black nylon tote bag, removing a small cellular device that would provide secure voice communication between Bailey and his boss, Conrad Billings. "Just attach the input plug to the phone adapter, then plug the phone into it like so. Pretty simple device, a hell of a lot better than what we were working with our first time out."

Taking the scrambler from Thornton, Bailey nodded his agreement. Within minutes he'd assembled the necessary components and was busy dialing Billings's number in Washington, D.C. After a few rings Calvin heard the receiver at the other end picked up, Conrad's gruff voice beating itself to death across a thousand miles of micro-thin wire. "Billings. This better be Calvin Bailey, who should have called an hour ago, or I'm gonna be highly pissed off."

Drowning a laugh, Bailey confirmed his identity with a quick password and a short series of numbers. "There. Now that you know it's me, all I'll add is that it's better to be pissed off than pissed on. What's the scoop? Thornton and the team are in mission prep right now; we'll be ready to infil around oh four hundred in the morning. Anything new from SOCOM?"

"Yeah, we got a burst from Chuikov on Foster's secure net. He left a set of coordinates for your DZ, and confirmed he's left the Fairbanks area. Foster's intelligence people pulled a map of the AO from their files and they said to tell you it's a twelve-second drop zone, fairly clear of obstacles, with a five-degree slope. You'll have trees ringing the DZ on three sides, a small stream on the fourth. No wires or radio towers, of course, the place he's picked to hide out in sits a hundred miles from the nearest village.

"NSA confirmed the dead Russian was a Spetsnaz commando assigned to the team of one Major Yuri Pushkin. Pushkin has dropped out of sight after being called to Moscow on the first thing smokin' out of Kabul. The girls at the FBI cracked our man in Valdez, and he's admitted to running an agent infiltration route for the last three years. He ID'd Chuikov as the man he'd brought over this last week, but it looks like the GRU set these routes up in single-man cells. There could be a parallel arrangement operating out of the same harbor for all we know.

"In short, I'd advise Bo to consider that a crack Spetsnaz team has been assembled and launched to track down Colonel Chuikov. Pushkin is a crackerjack soldier from what the NSA says, so much so he's suspected in at least five significant assassinations that have taken place around the world. We don't know if the two officers know each other personally, although it's a safe bet they're aware of each other's reputation. I'd consider Pushkin to be in Alaska already, either in Anchorage or Fairbanks, depending upon how good their network is operating."

Bailey sighed. Nothing was ever easy. "Did Foster give you the freq for the beacon? We'll need to program the plane's computers as well as our own device before getting airborne."

Billings rattled off a short frequency passed to him by Foster's efficient sergeant major. "By the way"—he paused after hearing Calvin confirm the numerics—"a Sergeant Major Stump says to tell Thornton hello for him. I don't know how the bastard tripped to Bo's being involved, but he did. Probably an old running buddy from Vietnam."

"I'll pass the word to Bo," replied Bailey. "If there's nothing else, we'd better get moving. Thornton says to tell you this will be our last contact until we bring Chuikov in. He wants the same financial and administrative arrangement for the team, to include Bannion and Lee, even though David isn't along for the ride this time out."

At the other end Billings rolled his eyes upward, figuring the amount in his head and knowing they'd have to pay it. One thing about Bo Thornton, he thought to himself, the man takes care of his people. Each one of the bastards was rapidly building up a substantial nest egg, money culled from assets seized from drug lords and their empires through the efforts of the DEA and other agencies. Thornton demanded the money paid to his team go untaxed, a command that had pissed the IRS off beyond reason until the president himself reviewed Springblade's impressive accomplishments and ordered it so. "Tell the madman it'll be taken care of; half the contract is already in the accounts mentioned, and Lee will get his, too. I can see me having to see the Man again about paying personnel not actually involved, but given the nature of the project I'm sure he'll sign off on it."

"Great, I'll pass it on to Bo. Anything else before we secure?"

Billings reached down and rubbed the soreness in his calf, where the doper's bullet had punched out a round hunk of living flesh during a recent crackhouse raid. The senior DEA official had in turn punched the shooter's lights out with a burst of high-velocity .22 Stingers, invoking Conrad's personal philosophy of maximum retaliation for even the slightest hint of an insult. "Tell the team Chuikov's information has been rated at the 'Q' level. What he can give us will set back Spetsnaz incursions at least ten years. Their potential wartime threat, based upon the nuggets Chuikov dropped in Foster's lap on their initial contact, has the Oval Office's asshole tighter than the vault door at Fort Knox. It seems the Russians could damn near bring chaos and disorder on a major level to Alaska within a seventy-two-hour time period through sabotage, assassination, and communications disruption. Chuikov reports over one hundred spec-war teams are targeted for infiltration into Alaska should the balloon go up. Forces Command would be at a loss to intercept maybe one percent of what would be swimming, boating, jumping, and crawling into the state. George wants Chuikov in D.C., regardless of cost."

"You got it, Toyota," rumbled Bailey. "By the way, you're starting to speak special-ops pretty good for a civilian."

Billings laughed, the soreness gone for now as he pulled his pants leg back down over the still-purple scar. "Have to, you gold-bricking son of a bitch. The more Springblade gets involved in, the more I find out what I don't know about guys like Thornton. Shit, I used to think Green Berets and SEALs were all crazy men, bits of Rambo and Chuck Norris wrapped up in a Clint Eastwood attitude. Since Alpine, though, and more so after that Bravo Sierra in Nicaragua, it's pretty obvious the Bo Thorntons of this world are every bit as professional as any doctor or lawyer. So I'm taking the time to learn the rap, gettin' tired of wondering what the hell a 'loach' or a 'blooper' or a 'SATCOM site' is."

Bailey felt a flood of affection wash over him as he listened to the man who was both his boss and friend. Billings was fighting the good fight and starting to feel like he was winning again. "Gotta go, boss. Bo's itching to get to the airfield, and we're on short numbers anyway. See you soon."

With a sharp click, the line between the two men went dead Dropping the government-issue black receiver on its cradle, Conrad Billings punched his intercom and ordered an appointment with the president. He was once again sending his best into harm's way and he didn't like the feeling any more now than when he'd done it the first time. From dopers to killers to turncoats and now Soviet commandos . . . when would Bo Thornton's wars ever end?

CHAPTER 14

Vasili Suworov dismissed his driver who was also the aging GRU marshal's personal bodyguard. The inner office in which he stood was comfortably warm, in contrast to the extreme bitter cold of the weather outside the slightly fogged windowpane overlooking Red Square. Where did summer go? he mused. Every once in a great while there would be a sudden chill like this, a cold front blown down from up north, off the steppes of Russia's open plains. Suworov hated the cold, a reminder of the war against Hitler and his armies so long ago. Twenty million dead Russians! They'd been bled dry, both in human lives and in human traits. The brutality of the war in Russia made those other conflicts in Korea, Afghanistan, and Vietnam pale in comparison. Russians knew what total war was all about; they knew what it took to win.

The GRU chief closed his mind's scrapbook of a war long over and returned to the conflict at hand. On his desk were the memos, faxes, and reports that had come in during the previous evening and early that morning. Between phone calls and reading, he barely had enough time to eat a quick lunch, *if* there wasn't a meeting or two scheduled with his key subordinates.

Right now he was obsessed with Pushkin's efforts to locate and terminate Peter Chuikov. The thought of such a senior Spetsnaz officer going over to the Americans galled him. Chuikov was more than just an officer, he was nearly a cult hero in the special-ops community. The man was an extraordinary example of intelligence, field craft, and sheer will. His missions had always been successful. How long had Chuikov been planning his defection? Suworov grimaced as a jet of sharp pain boiled up in his gut, the acids making themselves felt as he damned the colonel for the physical aggravation this mess was causing him.

Shifting through the neatly laid-out mounds of official documents, he soon separated those he wanted to review immediately from those which could wait. A small amount went into his trash bucket located beside the desk; others which could be delegated to his junior officers were so annotated. Seating himself in a chair taken from Goering's hunting palace in Germany at the war's end, Suworov noted without pleasure the depth of Chuikov's treachery. The microchips he'd removed from the GRU computers had been replaced with cleverly programmed clones, their data enough to fool the checks and balances built into the machines to detect the very kind of theft the colonel had engineered. If Pushkin could not intercept Chuikov before the Americans brought him in, the web of planned Spetsnaz operations in Alaska would be irrevocably jeopardized. Years of work, money, and planning would wind up on the desk of U.S. intelligence officials. Suworov could well imagine their shock when they began to unravel the enormous depth the Soviet penetration had made into the forty-ninth American state. Entire agent networks would be exposed, infiltration routes across the state into Canada would suddenly come to light, and massive caches of weapons, documents, money, and demolitions would be located, thanks to Chuikov's betrayal.

Vasili shook his gray-maned head in disgust. The human factor had raised its fickle finger once again, and Suworov knew from past experiences it was the human side of the equation that determined success or failure on a grand scale. The GRU grand master had to face reality: Pushkin might fail. There were certain networks and agents that could be saved or at least warned if Suworov moved quickly. Better they salvage what key operations/operatives they could than lose the entire effort by counting on five men, regardless of their skill and resourcefulness.

Taking up a heavy pen from the set on his desk, the fearsome head of Soviet intelligence began issuing orders. Certain caches would have to be recovered if possible, especially those located near American military bases and certain radar sites. Others of less importance yet still sensitive could be blown in place by teams of operatives on the GRU payroll. He'd insist on having several highly placed agents in the local government brought out, with a select few requiring termination simply because of the role they were to play if Soviet troops were to have launched a full-scale invasion. In short, the core of the spider's web needed to be saved. The loss would set GRU efforts back eight to ten years, meaning there would be a new man sitting at Suworov's desk before they were again ready. He would do what he could to make his successor's job easier, and just maybe the disaster at hand could be thwarted if Pushkin's team reached Chuikov first.

Dropping the ornate pen into its holder, he riffled through the reports before him, finally choosing a fax sent from a cutout in Anchorage the evening before. Scanning its contents, Suworov was pleased to see his agents were working overtime to assist Pushkin, who was already in Fairbanks sniffing out the colonel's trail. The GRU computer banks were working at a furious pace to track Chuikov's brazen use of the organization's credit cards, each recorded receipt a footprint in the colonel's path. Vasili noted the man's choice of equipment, indicating his decision to flee into the mountains, where he had room to maneuver. Chuikov couldn't risk the multitude of people in an urban environment. Anyone could be an agent or assassin on the GRU's payroll. Better to select the battleground if there was to be one and operate alone, which suited Peter Chuikov's training and personality. Suworov took a moment to imagine the ferocity of the battle should Pushkin's force meet the colonel's brand of singular combat. He ignored the American response, secure in the knowledge that Pushkin's team was a battle-hardened unit with recent experience and blooding in Afghanistan as well as in other remote wars of domination. The Americans would receive yet another bloody nose if they tangled with Spetsnaz. The thought brought a dour smile to the former Russian infantryman's deeply lined features.

Outside, a gust of wind blew through the square, its sound like that of a thousand moaning souls.

CHAPTER 15

Chuikov stripped the hare's skin from the now-still body in one fluid motion, discarding it in a hole he'd dug for that purpose. With a quick chop he removed the animal's head, four repeated cuts severing the beast's paws at the joint. Slipping the Swiss Army knife from the sheath at his side, he expertly gutted the rabbit, tossing what he wouldn't be using into the hole, which he covered using the camp knife's broad beam as if it were a shovel. He'd caught five of the big Alaskan hares using a simple snare he'd learned from marxist rebels in South Africa. Along with the river onions and roots he'd dug earlier, they'd make a marvelous stew—a meal fit for a wilderness king.

Hefting the bloody little beast's meaty remains in one hand, he dropped it into a plastic bag, which he then shoved into his day pack. Wiping the Rio Grande down with a large bandanna, Chuikov sheathed the massive blade, then cleaned the smaller pocket folder in much the same way. He was less than fifteen minutes from his camp, the snares placed along a game trail Chuikov had spotted while reconning the area the day before. His RON had been carefully prepared, a Gortex poncho of olive drab acting as a makeshift tent under which the colonel had laid his sleeping bag, rucksack, and weapons.

Always careful, Chuikov camouflaged the site so skillfully that a man would walk right past it, unaware of another's presence unless he literally stumbled over the tent. The Russian prepared his meals outside the camp's tiny perimeter, burning only the driest wood he could find in a small hole dug with the knife. If necessary he could smother the infant flames with one sweep of his hand, then disappear into the surrounding foliage. Water was not a problem; a small stream bubbled along less than thirty feet from where he slept. All in all it was an excellent place to rest and wait.

Tamping down the disturbed earth, Chuikov prepared to return to camp. He'd elected to carry the rifle in case he stumbled onto something worth killing at distance. The shotgun was hidden in a spot fifty meters upstream along with its spare shells, Chuikov remembering well the hard lessons learned after a lifetime of mortal combat. If he was right, the American team would be jumping in soon, his message to Foster explicit concerning the DZ's location and status. They would fly directly over his camp, alerting him as the pilot began his final approach so that the jump master could properly align the aircraft with the length of the clearing Chuikov had selected. Being the time of year it was, he doubted they would attempt to jump while it was dark; the chance of injury was too great for a mission of this importance. Of course they might not show at all, in which case he'd spend a few days getting the lay of the land, then begin humping for Canada.

Chuikov was certain Vasili Suworov would dispatch a team for him. The old goat couldn't let his actions go unpunished, especially since they would mean the dismantling of an entire operational front's plans. Spetsnaz itself would suffer as Chuikov had made microdot copies of the organization's entire Table of Organization and Equipment something Suworov couldn't know, since nothing would be found missing or tampered with at the office in question. No, the marshal would deploy the best Spetsnaz team he could muster, and the hunt would be unlike any Chuikov had conducted or been the quarry of.

Choosing to skirt a secondary game trail winding its way toward his campsite, Chuikov began the short hike back. All around him the woods were alive with light and freshness, the smell an aromatic blend of pine, fir, and a hundred varieties of meadow flowers. Moving with care, he picked his way through trees and scrub, sidestepping dead branches so as not to leave too obvious a trail. Just before reaching the tiny clearing he'd selected as home, the unmistakable murmur of an aircraft engine reached his sensitive ears.

Cocking his head slightly, Chuikov closed his eyes to concentrate on the sound. It seemed to be coming from the southwest, almost exactly in line with the approach the pilot had taken when he'd flown the colonel in. This plane was somehow different, though: larger, perhaps, two engines instead of the one. Striding to his tent, the Spetsnaz officer immediately began tearing down camp, quickly packing his belongings into the ruck. From the sounds the plane was making, Chuikov could tell it was landing, and that meant either someone else had chosen to visit this remote area, or that Suworov's warriors were far cleverer and closer than the colonel had imagined.

This wouldn't have surprised him at all. Professional soldiers of the warrior class were seldom surprised at anything their enemy might do. To avoid this weakness they trained rigorously, studied hard, and applied their knowledge whenever possible. The key to Spetsnaz operations was the element of surprise. Along with surprise came a level of angst, which annihilated the foe's ability to react effectively. Spetsnaz teams didn't feint, bob, or weave when they struck. Theirs was a critical knockout punch that landed first. Violence and speed characterized their assaults.

The plane's engines were suddenly silent. Chuikov finished packing, then retrieved the shotgun from its hiding place. Charging all his weapons, he made a careful search of the camp, intent on not leaving behind any telltale sign of his stay. A good tracker—and Spetsnaz possessed the best—would discover his lair sooner or later. But time was an ingredient Chuikov knew to be his most precious ally. He walked the area one more time just to be sure.

It was then that he heard the gunshot. Whether by accident or design, they had announced their arrival and intention. Chuikov realized the race for his life was once again under way. The Americans would not be on the ground for at least another fifteen hours, and even then he had no means to warn them of the danger. Checking his U.S. Forest Service map, Chuikov decided he would take the battle to the wolves first. Running would serve no purpose; there simply wasn't enough distance between him and his pursuers to make a difference. Spetsnaz troops were conditioned to run, hike, and jump like no other special forces. They would find his trail and lock on to it regardless of the time of day or weather. The Russian colonel realized his own vulnerability lay in the grid he'd elected to wall himself into until SOCOM could arrive. If he left that grid the Americans might never link up with him, especially if he were on the run. On the other hand Suworov's team could, and would pursue until he killed every last one of them, or they him. It was as if he were on a giant chessboard, a lonesome king facing the onslaught of a band of rooks and bishops whose goal was his eventual surrender or extinction. As in chess, then, he would not seek to escape or forestall his fate. The only alternative open to a king in such a situation is to attack. And so he would. With a wolfish grin the Soviet commando shed Peter Chuikov's newly formed image as a man of peace, replacing it with a form only his comrades in arms and the dead would instantly recognize as being the Peter Chuikov they all knew and feared.

Once again he was Spetsnaz.

Idiot! The pilot's attempt at flight once they'd landed had cost him his life, and the team the element of surprise. Worse, Pushkin had no idea where they had landed was indeed where Chuikov had requested to be taken. The tracker, whose name was Boris, was already searching for sign. Pushkin nodded in approval as the man carefully began where the plane had come to a stop, his full attention on the ground in front of him even as Antonov humped the body of the pilot back from where it had fallen.

"I am too good a shot, Yuri. The bullet shattered the bastard's spine, killing him instantly." Dropping the battered corpse at the major's booted feet, Antonov wiped from his hands the blood smeared across them. His assault rifle hung across his chest on its tactical sling like a guitar, the long barrel pointing downward.

"No matter, comrade, what's done is done. I only hope we instilled in this swine enough fear to fly us to where he dropped the colonel off yesterday. If not, the chase is all but over, as the trail ends here."

A sudden shout from Boris drew the two men's attention. The tracker was fifty feet away from the plane, kneeling and pointing at something only he could see. "A boot print here! There are others leading into the forest. He rested, the imprint of his backpack's frame clearly visible to me. We have him, Comrade Major, we have Colonel Chuikov!"

"He cannot be far, Yuri. No doubt he's heard the shot and is moving even now. What are your orders?"

Pushkin thought for only a moment before answering. "Shove the pilot's body into the cargo compartment before we move out. We'll leave the plane intact in case we need it to get out in a hurry. Igor can taxi it beneath that stand of trees at the south end of the strip.

"I want Boris up front, of course, you second, Igor, then myself, Kushkin at the rear. We chase one of our own so we must adopt tactics different from those Chuikov may be expecting. Everyone here served in Cambodia with the Khmer Rouge, a front Chuikov did not experience because of his assignments to Africa. We will adopt the small-unit tactics of the Rouge to confuse our colonel's attempts to engage us."

Antonov nodded sagely. "A wise move. Then you believe Chuikov will indeed consider coming against us?"

"Wouldn't you, Antonov? If the Americans are true to form, they will react slowly, with great caution and political stupidity. I believe we are the first to follow Colonel Chuikov to this point, and were I him it would be to my advantage to buy whatever time I could by meeting the enemy head on."

The plane's engines roared to life as Igor swung it around and raced down the grassy runway for the cover of the tree line. Kushkin, the second man attached to the major's team from Ryazan joined Boris, his teammate. The two of them exchanged information, then looked to Antonov for instructions. While the battle-savvy noncom met with them to explain Pushkin's orders, the major began running through his options. At most they had forty-eight hours in which to find, corner, and liquidate the target. Recovery of the chips was secondary, as Chuikov would be carrying them; of that Pushkin was sure. Even if he did manage to hide them during the chase, no one would recover the information they held, as it was Antonov's job to destroy the colonel's body entirely. Of course, should the Americans send a team in, things could change dramatically. Pushkin chose not to underestimate the possibility of their coming under fire from another factor in the equation. Unlike Suworov, whose estimate of American special operations was quite low,

Pushkin knew them to be formidable enemies. He'd seen the results of American-sponsored forays against even Spetsnaz teams while serving in Afghanistan, and he still shuddered at how grisly the battle scenes had appeared after being discovered. No, they needed to push a confrontation with Chuikov and settle the matter as soon as possible.

"We're ready, Yuri." Antonov was standing beside his leader and friend, his face painted in long streaks of black and green to match the pattern of his woodland uniform.

"Good. Everyone is to maintain his distance, hand and arm signals only. We must move at a pace that will close the distance between our prey and ourselves, but keep in mind I am trusting to Chuikov to make his presence known first. We have only so much ammunition, so make your shots count if we are engaged, and be wary of booby traps. The colonel is a master of the unsuspected."

"He has at least a rifle, Comrade Major. I found the imprint of its butt plate next to where he laid his pack."

The team nodded. Chuikov's skill as a marksman was equal to that of Pushkin. Their hackles began to quiver as they remembered they were standing in the middle of a rough-out airstrip, the closest cover several hundred feet away. Reading their thoughts, Pushkin put them at ease. "Relax a bit. If the colonel were within rifle shot we would all be dead. I suggest we not tempt fate, though. Boris, be so kind as to get our asses out of here, would you?"

With a smile the Spetsnaz manhunter turned and began loping toward the woodline, his eyes like a hawk's as he swept the nearing patch of thin trees for signs of ambush. Behind him the team began to stagger their interval, each man's rifle pointing in an opposite direction to provide an instant response to any fire from the flanks. Pushkin allowed the adrenaline rush of the chase to course through his well-conditioned body, the surge exploding within him, cleansing his mind of stray thoughts and concerns. Somewhere ahead of them was Chuikov, a master of individual tactics and deception. He was easily the most dangerous man Pushkin had been asked to kill, and just as easily the most capable of killing the major himself. Ahead of him Antonov turned and smiled, the look in the senior noncom's eyes telling Pushkin that he, too, felt the thrill of battle coming on. What would happen to a man like his Sergeant Major Antonov once his age crept up on him, stealing away his energy and lightninglike reactions?

Pushkin pushed the thought from his mind as quickly as it had emerged. Boris was inside the false safety of the trees now, with Igor and Antonov spreading out behind him to cover their flanks. A quick glance to his rear told the Russian commander that their rear security was in place and doing his job, the man's head and eyes rotating in unison as he monitored their back trail as well as the tree limbs above him. The forest's floor was clear of deadfall, its surface a carpet of tender mosses and fallen leaves. The earth soaked up their footfalls like a massive shock absorber, only the rasping of an occasional twig or bush rubbing against the soft cotton of their uniforms disturbing the natural quiet of the forest.

Up front the point man's hand suddenly appeared, its message indicating a halt as Boris determined which way

Chuikov had turned after leaving the airstrip. The team was held in check for another ten minutes as they adjusted themselves to the new environment. Their hearing became more acute as the unique sounds of the woods sorted themselves out. Eyesight sharpened, as each sound demanded a close look for future identification. By the time Boris raised himself from where he'd been patiently kneeling, the team was in tune with their environment. Now the pace was slower, more careful, as Boris had to work harder to keep them on track. Soon they would come into contact with their former comrade; soon they would pit their collective skill against one man's will to survive.

CHAPTER 16

The art of LALO (low altitude–low opening) was first introduced by the Soviets, when they ordered the cream of their airborne forces to jump from perfectly good airplanes into huge snowdrifts. Unfortunately the partisans resisting the invasion of their soil by Russia's militaristic government of expansion had received word of the impending attack and buried hundreds of boulders in the snowy landing zones selected by the Russian commander.

The ensuing airdrop had a profound impact on Russian airborne ops from that day forward.

LALO operations weren't fully appreciated until the Rhodesians began experimenting with parachutes that were opened by a smaller chute attached above the primary canopy. This first chute would literally pull the primary open, allowing immediate canopy inflation upon the jumper's exit from the aircraft. Combat drops of as low as one hundred fifty feet were accomplished using this method, putting troops on the ground in remote areas with the least amount of warning to the enemy.

American LALO ops received a boost when the "Charlie" -model parachute was introduced into the airborne inventory. This canopy was of thicker stock than the Dash-1 Bravo, a factor that dramatically decreased the rate of descent of a paratrooper wearing full equipment when jumping from combat altitudes of five hundred feet. Designed for combat-altitude drops, the Charlie model served equally as well at two hundred and fifty feet, an elevation which was danger-close yet extremely practical for covert infiltrations.

Thornton sat in the seat nearest the closed rear ramp of the C-7A Caribou. On his head the he wore an issue Kelvar helmet, its parachutist safety webbing secured snugly down the sides of his face and around his chin. He, as well as the rest of the team, wore lightweight battle-dress fatigues and jungle boots. Balanced across his upper legs was a fully packed Alice rucksack, its frame well padded since he wouldn't have the opportunity or time to lower it once he left the airframe. Thornton's web gear carried six magazine pouches, two canteens, a first-aid kit, a holster for the Glock, one magazine pouch, and a sheath knife. The knife was a gift from Bill Buchman, an Oregon knife maker who'd met Thornton while vacationing in Cannon Beach. Ground from a high-quality stain-resistant steel, the knife's blade was a full seven inches long with a sharpened false edge. The beautifully contoured handle slabs were shaped from ironwood, each pinned and epoxied into position so that they appeared to be one with the full-length steel tang. Thornton had lost his beloved Randall in Nicaragua, so the present from Buchman was a timely event.

Slung over each man's shoulder was a Colt Commando, its barrel pointed down and receiver reversed, as prescribed for airborne operations. Each Springblader had elected to slap a twenty-round magazine into his weapon's well, knowing he might have to come up firing on the ground. Thornton checked the tie-down strap fastened loosely below his right knee, then touched the black barrel of the Russian ballistic knife hanging from a cordura quick-draw sheath on his battle harness. If necessary, he could cut himself free of his parachute harness with the knife should the DZ be too hot to worry about undoing snaps and lines.

The ballistic was a trophy taken off a Soviet paratrooper in Afghanistan during one of Thornton's unrecorded deployments to that country. Ordered to avoid combat, the Green Beret had realized his expertise would never be taken seriously unless he not only worked, but fought alongside the fierce mountain warriors who were his hosts. It was during one of these unauthorized forays that Thornton encountered a team of Russian special forces sent to assassinate key figures within the freedom fighters' organization. In a murderous frenzy of hand-to-hand combat, Thornton found himself squaring off with a para who tried unsuccessfully to use the Spetsnaz-issued knife on him. For his troubles, Ivan bought a belly full of Randall-made steel, and Thornton adopted the Russian's strange battle blade as his own.

Seated next to Thornton was Mike Bannion, who'd joined the team just hours before they lifted off from Elmendorf. Bannion was a SLAM operative, and a favorite with the team he'd joined while they were protecting Ricardo Montalvo in San Francisco. The former SEAL had the rugged good looks of a pro linebacker and the combat intensity of Audie Murphy. A close friend of Jason's, Mike Bannion was a welcome replacement for David Lee, who was still out of action due to wounds received when he and Thornton had taken on Angel Barahone several months back. Frank Hartung was next in the stick, this jump being his 2,500th static line blast since he'd joined the Army over thirty years ago. Hartung's face betrayed no concern over what he considered just another way to get to the ground. The sergeant major had personally inspected each man's equipment both prior to and after it had been donned, as well as walking the entire length of the aircraft to ensure its proper rigging for a LALO operation.

Calvin Bailey looked over at Jason Silver, elected to push the stick once Thornton, the jump master, left the aircraft's rear ramp. Silver was busy adjusting one of his three Moeller throwing knives, a tool he was an expert with. Bailey recalled seeing the results of one of Silver's throws, a guard who'd sucked down a windpipe full of flashing steel at the San Francisco Zoo during the rescue of Montalvo's beautiful daughter, Maritza. "Two-fifty ain't much altitude," yelled Calvin across the space separating the two men. "Been a while since I've seen the ground up that close."

Silver nodded, the heavy beat of the Caribou's engines making conversation strained at best. "Me, Bo, and the Old Man did three of these while we were in Coronado. All over the ocean, a nice blast! Probably be rocks and shit on this DZ coming up! Watch your feet and knees and keep your elbows in close! Otherwise you're liable to get all eight kinds of fucked up!''

Fixing the team's demo wizard with a stare that could freeze water, Bailey wondered why he'd brought the subject up in the first place. For his part, Silver was completely at ease with the upcoming jump. He'd loved the feel of his knees in the breeze from the moment they'd dropped him from the tower at Benning. Jason Silver didn't think of jumping as a hazardous part of his job as a soldier. Instead, he considered it one of life's good fortunes that the Army hadn't figured out how to louse up for the enlisted man. Whether from 250 feet, or 25,000, Jason Silver was an Airborne Ranger all the way, all day, hard-core in every way.

The Caribou had been flying north for nearly two hours when the Air Force crew chief leaned over and gave Thornton double tens, meaning they were twenty minutes out from the DZ. Bo nudged Bannion, who'd fallen asleep, making sure the agent was awake before he passed the hand signal down. With a grunt Mike acknowledged the information, popping his right hand open and shut four times for Hartung's benefit. Without hesitation the sergeant major shook Bailey awake, mouthing, ''Twenty minutes!'' as he pumped both hands twice. Calvin, turning to Silver, received a curt nod from the former Ranger, who was already beginning an equipment check.

There's a subtle glimmer of dread that shoots through you when the realization wells up in your guts that you're about to throw yourself out of an airplane at altitude. Dread and a perverse thrill twist around the core of your being as you mentally begin to examine all the straps, hooks, and snaps that make up your equipment. Helmets are adjusted, brims touched lightly to make sure the hundred-mile-an-hour tape is molded like a glove around the sharp edges of the polymer brain bucket. Static lines are gently tugged, and the hook attaching you to the plane's steel cable is opened and closed to ensure its proper functioning. Rucksack straps are cinched down for the fifth or sixth time. Lowering lines are located, release straps checked to make sure you can activate them once you're in the air and under a full canopy. Some men prefer to wear thin Nomex aviator's gloves to protect their hands during landing, others elect to adjust high-impact HALO goggles around their eyes. After the twenty-minute warning a whole new attitude blows through the aircraft; you can feel its weight pushing you against the red-webbed seat supporting your now-puckering asshole.

Ten minutes out the huge ramp began opening, hydraulic motors whining like scalded dogs as they slowly lowered the platform into position. A curious blend of warm-cool air rushed over the team as they watched the crew chief toss them a thumbs-up, indicating everything was perfect for the drop from the pilot's viewpoint. Six minutes out Thornton stood up, bracing himself against the side of the aircraft as the crew chief hooked his static line up. With his back to the bird's open maw, Bo yelled, "Six minutes!" down at his fellow jumpers, his hands pushed forward at chest level in the classic jump-master pose. With the exquisite timing of a professional musician, Thornton brought the team to its feet, hooked them up, checked their equipment, and watched them slap each other on the ass with a hearty "All okay!" which made its way up the line until Bannion roared the confirmation directly into Thornton's grinning face.

God, how he loved the Airborne.

Turning to the crew chief, Thornton gave his own thumbs-up. Hooked by a long cable to the aircraft's internal communication net, the man informed the pilot they were standing in the door. Receiving the long-awaited nod, Thornton gingerly shuffled his way onto the ramp, his right hand clutching the yellow static line in an inverted bite so it wouldn't flop around in the turbulence now buffeting the interior of the plane. Bo felt Bannion snuggle up behind him, the agent's rucksack bumping the backs of his thighs as Mike struggled to maintain his balance. They would exit the ramp by simply walking off it at a slight angle, handing the static lines off to the crew chief, who would control them as each man dropped off the ramp's edge.

Because he was the first jumper, Thornton handed his static line off, placing both hands in front of him so that his elbows were held in tight. They carried no reserve parachutes, the equipment unnecessary since a reserve wouldn't have time to open at this altitude should the primary chute fail. It was only then that Thornton looked directly out the rear of the speeding aircraft, his throat tightening as he watched the heavily wooded terrain of Alaska's pristine wilderness rushing underneath him at one hundred knots per hour. Jumping at altitude was risky enough, but at least there was some reaction time built in should something go wrong. A LALO drop put a jumper on the ground inside a limited drop zone within seven seconds of the chute exploding open behind him.

It was a hair-raising experience, with no room for error allowed.

Thornton hadn't even realized he was moving when the green light punched into his consciousness like a sharp piece of rounded jade. Suddenly his feet were above his head as the slipstream ripped at his tightly coiled body, whipping and snapping it until the static line yanked the chute free of its tray. With a wicked pop, the canopy blossomed open, the shock riveting Thornton's jaws together as his shoulders and crotch took the bulk of the system's punishment. Whipping his arms and hands upward to gain control of the parachute's steering toggles, Bo forced himself to wedge his feet and knees together in anticipation of the landing he knew was coming. With an audible grunt he hammered into the DZ, rolling and twisting as he had been trained to do so long ago at Fort Benning. Coming to his feet, the veteran of more jumps than he cared to recall began running around the still-inflated parachute, collapsing it as the sound of his companions' equally brutal landings erupted on all sides of his own impact point. In seconds it was over, the quiet of the predawn morning enveloping them as they rushed to control their breathing, jamming the silk chutes and nylon harnesses into canvas kit bags they'd cache in a common grave off the drop zone.

In the distance they could hear the Caribou's engines fading away much like the semidarkness they'd jumped into. Seconds later the friendly drone was replaced with the crashing sounds of gunfire opposite the aircraft's direction of flight. Chuikov was obviously having problems of his own, and Thornton knew what the solution would be.

Cold steel and hot lead at close range, because that's the way he liked it.

CHAPTER 17

He'd backtracked nearly half the distance to the landing field, careful to stay within the protection of the trees and brush along the way. The last thing he wanted was a head-on confrontation with the Spetsnaz point man, no matter how successful he might be at getting the drop on his former comrade in arms. Odds were odds, and those odds would get him killed.

Chuikov found the spot he was looking for, a small crevice broken out from a cluster of heavy boulders to the left and just above the trail he'd made the day before. Easing up along the backside of the jumbled mass, he cached his ruck under a low-growing shrub, taking the scoped rifle as he continued into the maze of stone and dirt. A slight breeze, funneled through the moss-covered outcropping, fanned his bearding face. The Russian, in the best tradition of Spetsnaz, felt glorious despite the danger now coming at him. Chuikov had lived for the hunt all his life; he was at home with a rifle in his hands and the smell of the bush clinging to his clothes.

The crevice petered out onto a narrow rock ledge, which the Russian had to wiggle onto in order to cover the avenue of approach he knew the team chasing him would have to use. Unsheathing the M-77, Chuikov dropped the scope cover back into the crevice, where he could retrieve it later. Quietly sliding the rifle's bolt back a fraction of a hair, he confirmed that there was a round in the Ruger's chamber. Chuikov had selected Nosler partition ammunition in Anchorage because of its worldwide reputation as a big-game round of tremendous reliability. The .223 was a common-sense choice for this situation; its velocity and accuracy a winning combination on the battlefield.

Imagining what his position looked like from the front, Chuikov began molding his body into the dips and hollows offered by the natural shooting platform. Carefully slipping a long, wide piece of camouflaged netting from a generous cargo pocket on his pants leg, he draped it over his head and shoulders, taking great pains to slip it down along the rifle's upper receiver group and scope in order to break up both his and the weapon's distinctive outline. The netting was porous enough so that his field of view was unobstructed.

As a further precaution he unsnapped the leather strap holding the big Rio Grande camp bowie in place, slipping the wide-bellied knife up alongside him just in case an unheard visitor managed to get in behind his roost. Chuikov had blackened the highly polished blade using the charcoal from his tiny cooking fires. A knife this large was a practical camp implement, but in combat, under the right circumstances, its brilliant blade would telegraph a man's location for miles. He could feel the Beretta on his side, the 9-mm cocked, locked, and ready for action.

It wasn't long before he heard them coming. It wasn't that Pushkin and his men weren't quiet; they were. It was the silence the forest took on as they made their approach through it which alerted the waiting marksman. Animals quit their busy woodland activities; the squirrels Chuikov had been half watching suddenly darted up tall trees, thick gray tails at attention as they swept the area below them with telescopic eyes. Birds became silent. Even the wind stalled in the trees, an unnoticed heat broiling up from the floor of the forest, sending long, salty rivulets of sweat down Chuikov's forehead and cheeks.

They had to be close, he thought to himself. But where? Falling into habits honed by hours of patient waiting, he relied on his peripheral vision, sweeping the area to his front and sides in slow arcs, varying their depths as his mind recorded distance, lighting, shading, possible cover and concealment, and . . . movement!

A flicker really, nothing more. A brief glimpse of activity where before there had been none. Chuikov lowered his head behind the scope, resting his right cheek against the Ruger's walnut brown stock. Peering through the optic, he focused his attention in the area where he'd spotted his quarry, clearing his mind so that his eye's messages wouldn't be confused with what his thoughts might wish him to believe. There it was again! Only this time Chuikov had a fix on the source. Damn! he thought. They were closer than he'd realized, which meant they were far better than he was giving them credit for. Vasili indeed had sent a top-notch team to hang his hair from a pole. Chuikov would have liked to have known who the officer leading this handpicked band was.

The commando was kneeling, a black AR-15 rifle gripped in his hands, his uniform American-issue camouflage. "They've been to a cache," he whispered to himself. "Full compliment of weapons and supplies, everything stamped 'Made in the USA.' " Chuikov tried to define the man's features, hoping to possibly identify him. If he could, the Russian might have an inkling as to who was on his trail. The attempt proved to be impossible.

Fighting off the urge to center-punch the Spetsnaz commando between the running lights, he allowed his scope to drift right, then left, searching for the whereabouts of the other commandos. A pucker of movement twelve or so meters to the first soldier's immediate right exposed a second infiltrator. Chuikov was unable to pinpoint his location because of the trees masking the man's further forward travel. They were moving in a formation totally foreign to Chuikov's experience, making it difficult for him to gauge where one might be in relation to another. It was obvious the team leader had studied his target well, marking Chuikov's weaknesses while trying to stay as far away from his strengths as possible.

The Soviet colonel felt the hairs rising along the back of his neck. It appeared he might have walked into a trap, his confidence in being able to predict his enemy's movements and thinking proving now to be an exercise in smugness. Should there be a commando already ahead of him, the man might easily cut Chuikov's second trail leading to his present position. That would put his rear in danger of being blocked off unless he were to vacate the hideout immediately. The company of at least two Spetsnaz headhunters to his front dissolved any hope Chuikov had of slithering off the ledge without being spotted, his flanks consisting of an open space and a short jump to the ground at either end of the ledge.

Chuikov was all dressed up with no place to go, and he didn't like the feeling one damned bit.

There was the chance the Russian team would slip past his hiding spot, missing him completely. If so, the colonel might strike the battle's initial blow as he'd wanted to all along. The trick would be to remain absolutely still, praying the man on point would be so absorbed in yesterday's trail that he would miss whatever sign Chuikov had left while backtracking. If the commandos bypassed him, he could drop back onto *their* trail and possibly take at least one man out of the equation facing him. For fifteen minutes the Russian willed himself to become part of the stone surrounding him. There were no sounds from the narrow opening behind him, and the returning sounds of the forest assured him his hunters were now well past his lair.

Now Chuikov would become the hunter.

Moving quickly but without haste, he slid rearward into the crevice's opening, bending to snatch up the scope cover as he high-stepped back toward the rocky entrance. Taking several moments to visually as well as audibly recon the forest surrounding the stone structure, Chuikov convinced himself the Spetsnaz team had missed his trail entirely. Slinging the rifle, he made sure the bowie's safety strap was in place, then began trailing the men ahead of him. It wasn't long before he caught a look at the tail gunner's broad back before it disappeared into a dense barrier of gooseberry bushes. The colonel allowed a trace of a smile to rent his grim mask, the handle of the Rio Grande imprisoned within the powerful grip of his right hand as he withdrew it from the leather sheath at his side.

The art of military stalking is as difficult to teach a soldier as is the skill of hitting a target with a rifle at one thousand meters. Chuikov was a perfectionist when it came to shadowing his intended prey, exhibiting a level of awareness and patience uncommon even for Spetsnaz personnel. He could attune himself to not only his immediate environment, but with the "vibes" sent off from the man or woman being targeted. Because of this skill he was able to move both quickly and silently, plunging himself into nonexistence whenever he felt the rhythm of the hunt faltering.

The team's scheme of maneuver was now quite clear to him. It was a clever variation of Chinese small-unit tactics, probably picked up by the Vietnamese or Cambodians and adapted to their particular needs. In this case the tail gunner was positioned further back than most Western infantry squad leaders would like, a move which was meant to allow the last man in the formation an opportunity to spot and interfere with an ambush that may have been kept in check until the target was either within the kill zone, or walking into a much larger KZ. It was also meant to warn any other troops moving behind a vanguard element of impending danger, and Chuikov knew it to be a viable tactic. Here, though, it merely meant one man was out of touch with his comrades for no good reason. Chuikov was but one man, not a squad or platoon. He could never hope to initiate a successful ambush against a team, not having the numbers or proper weaponry to pull it off. The tail gunner could be used as a maneuver element against the colonel *if* he were to be contained by the other members of the team until such an action could be brought into play, but that meant leaving the rear vulnerable to being taken out because of a break in contact.

Which was exactly what had happened.

Chuikov slipped like a phantom behind the struggling soldier, electing to work parallel to the trooper as he tried to remain quiet, move quickly, and stay alert all at the same time. It was futile task, even for someone as experienced as the man obviously was. Chuikov sunk to his hands and knees, moving underneath the natural barriers placed in their way while the other man was forced to claw, slip, force, and push his way through. The colonel knew someone up ahead would notice the problem sooner or later and would signal for a halt until the tail gunner was once again in sight. He would have to move quickly, execute his plan, and be gone before the team leader sent someone back to find their lost comrade.

Kushkin was pissed. He'd lost sight of the major nearly five minutes ago, making half-assed eye contact with the man for less than a second before the forest swallowed them both up. He could hear someone moving off to his right flank, although whoever it might be was far out in front of the team's tail-end Charlie. Once Pushkin caught on to the fact that his rear security was stumbling around lost the man would throw a fit. Kuchkin's professional pride was at stake, so he pushed himself faster than he would otherwise, seeking a hole in the entangling mass of branches and small trees cutting the Spetsnaz veteran off from his friends.

Suddenly he froze as the sound of a branch snapping reached his ears. It had come from his left and it was closer than Kushkin liked. Slowly pivoting his body so that the automatic rifle he was holding swung in line with his vision, the commando prepared to release a burst of .223 fireballs into whatever might be creeping alongside him. Another snap, then a scuttle nearly caused the Russian to bear down on the trigger for all he was worth. Kushkin stopped himself as a fat squirrel bounded up a nearby tree, stopping to scold him mightily.

Releasing a ball of pent-up air from his lungs, the soldier slipped the weapon's barrel downward, wiping a sweating hand against his cotton trousers. Fucking animals! he raged to himself. The last thing he needed to do was blow the whole operation by shooting up a rodent. Pushkin would skin him alive while Antonov was stepping on his balls with those great large feet of his. The thought made Kushkin involuntarily shudder to himself at how his life could have ended so far from his village in Mother Russia.

And then it did.

Chuikov froze. He'd seen the furry animal at the exact moment it had spotted him. For an instant the Russian stalker had hoped he hadn't startled the squirrel, a hope which proved to be wishful thinking when the beast turned and scampered away from their encounter, snapping a dry stick in the wake of his flight. The colonel closed his eyes in expectation of the wad of lead he knew would be coming his way when the commando began spraying rifle bullets into the ground and trees around him. A second later the colonel opened them, understanding the man had identified the squirrel a millisecond before he'd opened fire. Chancing a sideways glance at the once-again-moving trooper, Chuikov scuttled forward the last three meters to his objective. Once at the base of the tree he stood straight up, keeping the thick pine's trunk between Kushkin and himself. The bowie was already in his hand, its cutting edge facing outward in lustful expectation of the orgy of blood and tissue it would soon be feeding upon.

Chuikov had learned over the years that using a knife to remove sentries was an encounter best solved by either avoiding the guard in the first place, or with another weapon besides a blade. Too many things could go wrong using a knife, including cutting oneself during the actual execution of the target. He'd never favored this approach to sentry disenrollment, preferring the excellent suppressed weapons in the GRU's armory over cold steel.

If there was a method that worked, Chuikov knew it to be perhaps the simplest and most direct application of a knife ever developed by the martial side of primitive man. You just chopped the bastard's head off. Of course you needed a knife of sufficient size and weight to do that, something ordinary bayonets and combat knives lacked in both areas. Chuikov addressed the grip on his bowie, feeling the heft of the mighty knife as he choked up on the rosewood grips. Now, *this* was a blade made for hacking and hewing, he thought. One well-placed blow with the Rio Grande's rolled edge would easily decapitate a man, cleaving through his hat, collar, any jewelry around his neck, or an errant leather rifle sling without a problem.

Of course decapitation was a messy affair, and Chuikov was certain to get splattered by the fountain of hot blood that would spew up from the headless corpse's open stump as soon as the bowie sliced its way through the major artery and attending veins between the base of the skull and upper chest area.

He'd live with it.

Kushkin tramped past the massive pine without a second glance. He heard the squirrel high above him continuing to hurl insults, making the soldier long for the luxury of being able to blow the little sucker's guts out with a single round from the American assault rifle. The Russian looked up, hoping to catch sight of the tiny angry face and perhaps scare the noisy bastard just a little bit more when he heard the unmistakable crunch of a boot behind him.

The squirrel's continuing chatter gave Chuikov his opening. As the tail gunner's head rotated upward the colonel stepped out from behind the far side of the tree so that he was now directly behind the already-reacting soldier. His arm was cocked fully back, the knife at a slight angle and gripped firmly in his callused hand. With his free hand held out for balance, the Russian swung the knife forward with all the power his warrior's spirit could muster. The ten-inch carbon-steel blade caught the soldier at the base of the neck on the right side, splitting the first several layers of skin and pile-driving into the built-up muscles protecting the neck and throat as if they were dry reeds. The man's hands opened up in an automatic reflex to the thousands of nerves being disjoined by the heavy combat blade's arc, his rifle falling free, swinging at waist level due to the sling's precarious attachment around Kushkin's now-shredded lower neck. Chuikov's brain registered the sudden pumping of the commando's shoulders, their breadth rising and falling like meaty pistons as the splintered spinal cord began transmitting a multitude of errant messages throughout the dying body.

As expected, a jet spray of rich arterial blood exploded from Kushkin when the Rio Grande parted the man's jugular. Great, steady waves of iron-rich gore splattered everything within reach of the mightily pumping heart's efforts, soaking Chuikov's face and upper body with its sticky influence. The knife exited Kushkin's neck without slowing down, its blade bathed in a sheen of body fluids and microscopic bits of bone and still-living tissue. Stepping back to prepare for a second blow downward, Chuikov watched the trooper's head jump crazily into the air, the last vestiges of life in the man's eyes piercing the colonel's soul as the hairy ball spun away into the woods. Stopping himself in mid-stroke, Chuikov stepped farther back as Kushkin's body collapsed rearward, nearly striking the colonel as it whumped into the soft mattress of pine needless, twigs, and moss on which they stood. A final burp of type-A-positive blood was belched forth from the gaping neck wound, its impact splattering Chuikov's dusty jungle boots. Shit! he thought as he spun around and quickly began slipping through the stand of trees. That's *all* I needed!

Behind him he could hear men working their way back

through the forest in search of their missing teammate. The squirrel, its shrill voice muted as it watched Chuikov's violence from the safety of a thick limb, began howling as the first Russian reached the remains at the base of the tree. Without a moment's hesitation Antonov turned, lifted his rifle to his shoulder, and blew the impudent little nut stuffer away with one well-placed shot.

Chuikov began running for his life.

CHAPTER 18

Pushkin ordered a wagon-wheel perimeter around the body of their dead comrade. While Antonov strip-searched Kushkin's remains for anything that could tie the corpse to the GRU, the other three maintained a silent watch over the forest around them. "He's clean," whispered the Spetsnaz veteran. "The only thing missing is his wolf's-head necklace."

Pushkin snorted. "Naturally! Chuikov has taken it as a trophy for himself while at the same time issuing us a challenge. The wolves are fighting amongst themselves, just as in nature. I will give our colonel credit, though. He drew first blood."

"Which tells us several things, doesn't it?"

"Yes, Antonov. It surely does. We now know that Chuikov is definitely here, that the American team is not on the ground yet, and that the colonel will not be content to hide from us until they arrive."

Boris, his pride stinging, as it was he who should have

discovered Chuikov's presence before Kushkin's fatal encounter, grumbled from where he lay. "It was foolish for him to attack us. We may never have found him before the Americans arrived. I had heard Colonel Peter Chuikov was a smart man, now I am not so sure."

Pushkin paused, allowing his eyes to rove the treetops overlooking the small group. Damn Chuikov! he cursed. The bastard could be drawing a bead on any one of them right now, given his skill with a rifle. Pushkin needed to get his men moving while the trail was so hot it was smoking. At the same time he needed their confidence rebuilt, the blatant killing of Kushkin devastating to the team's morale. "Our colonel struck because no matter his betrayal of our homeland he is Spetsnaz. It goes against his grain to run when he has the means to fight.

"Also, it may be that the Americans will abandon him, believing his information to be of no value and his defection a hoax. Chuikov has no assurance he will be recovered, that is why he came here in the first place. Should no rescue team show up he possesses freedom to maneuver, and Canada is not that far away for a man used to walking."

Antonov nodded his head in agreement. "It could also be that the Americans are not due for a while. If they were already here or coming soon, Chuikov would lie low. Exposing himself in that case would only decrease his chances of getting out in one piece.

"On the other hand, if he hurt us or caused us to be more cautious in our pursuit, then a bold move would be prudent."

Pushkin sighed. "You are right, as usual, Sergeant Major. Then we must overcome this setback and press onward. The only way the Americans can get in is to either land an aircraft or parachute from one. Until we hear engines it is just us and the colonel. Time, now more than ever, is of the essence."

Antonov took his cue from Pushkin, pointing at Boris, who was lying closest to him. "Comrade, you are on point again. Our lives are in your hands, as is the accomplishment of the mission. We must travel as quickly as possible while Chuikov's scent is strong enough to follow. At the same time exercise all caution. Remember, the man we hunt is of our own stock. If he is successful a second time we will begin to lose what edge we have over him."

The tracker rose, a hard glint of professional pride burning in his eyes. "We must keep him on the defensive, then, moving in haste, unable to stop to eat or rest."

"Correct," affirmed Pushkin. "Antonov will be second, then myself and Igor. Do not forget Chuikov's long gun and his skill with it. Why he took such a chance by getting this close to Kushkin I don't know, but I am certain he won't attempt such a feat again. Chuikov is now buying time. He will run toward where he expects to meet the Americans, so we must overtake our quarry or risk a confrontation with a force perhaps larger than the four of us. Questions?"

There were none. Without looking back, the Soviet commandos began jogging after their tracker, whose steady gait was one they could maintain all day and well into the night if necessary.

Except that night never really fell in the Land of the Midnight Sun.

CHAPTER 19

It seemed to Peter Chuikov he'd been wearing the uniform of a Spetsnaz soldier all his life. Thinking back on it, he couldn't put his finger on exactly what had made him begin questioning the direction his life was taking. Perhaps like a great journey there were a thousand little steps that all led to that final destination, a destination sometimes not imagined or conceived of when the first step was taken.

Chuikov remembered its beginning as if it were twenty minutes ago instead of twenty years. His father, a member of the party and veteran of the war, had come home with a huge smile on his face. Taking the young man aside, he'd informed him of his appointment to officers' school, with Spetsnaz training an opportunity should he do well while earning his commission. "Take an old soldier's word for it, Peter. The army treats its officers well if they learn the ropes and play the game. An enlisted man is like a rug; he's there to provide comfort and to be walked over."

Chuikov heard his father's words and believed them. He'd known older friends and schoolmates who'd been privileged to enter the various services at rank. Some, a very few, had gone on to Spetsnaz training. The ones who didn't make the grade made more of an impression on the boy than those who had. They came back looking as if they'd spent time in one of the camps Peter's father had helped to liberate in Nazi Germany. Not allowed to discuss their ordeal, the young men would keep to themselves, their bodies as well as spirit broken over the rack called Spetsnaz.

Still, Chuikov yearned to attend the dreaded selection course. He studied hard in officers' school, climbing to the top of his class with a string of impressive scholastic victories. On the playing field he was soon respected, then feared. Classmates watched as a transformation took place—the innate ability inside Peter Chuikov to soldier and lead coming to the surface under the harsh environment of military training. Also watching Chuikov were his instructors, men whose jobs it was to scout out new talent for Soviet special operations. Russia had always been intrigued with black warfare, this obsession sparking the birth of Spetsial'naya Naznacheniya, or Spetsnaz.

Designed to carry out missions against an enemy's very heart, Spetsznaz commandos were expected to be men of iron. Their training was brutal, designed to cull the weak-willed and physically incapable from the ranks with all due speed. Those who volunteered for Spetsnaz either made the grade or didn't. There existed no second chances or medical recycles for men who couldn't conquer themselves and the trials of the Higher Airborne Command School at Ryazan. It was here that Peter Chuikov was sent upon being commissioned, and it was here that he found a home.

Spetsnaz, he discovered, was created primarily with the intention of allowing Russia to seek out and destroy her enemies' atomic weapons before such devices could be launched against the motherland. Its teams were expected to operate without support from the Red Army and were frankly not given much chance of returning from their missions unless they possessed such strength and skill that no one could stand in their way. As the organization grew into the 1960s, its mission statement became layered. Soviet doctrine adopted the position that "weapons" also included key enemy personnel, and not necessarily those who wore military uniforms. Soon political assassination and murder became an aspect of Spetsnaz training, the goal to deny the enemy the means to conduct war at any level within his own borders. Without people to make decisions for them, the masses would falter, then fall. A successful war depended upon swift action and concrete planning. It was the job of the Spetsnaz commando to deny these key ingredients to his enemy, to coerce him into submission and defeat by any means available, using Soviet tactics with the utmost violence and terror possible to achieve a state of paralysis.

To this one-two punch there was added a kick. Spetsnaz teams would also seek out and destroy enemy lines of communication, transportation, and energy. They would dismantle a country's ability to move its supplies and people during war, cut off the capability to inform and alert, thereby isolating and separating states into zones, which could then be mopped up by regular Soviet forces. Hence an enemy would be toppled, losing his leadership, weaponry, and ability to support himself within days if not hours.

To accomplish this, the Soviet high command gave the formation of Spetsnaz high priority. Satisfied with their positive experiences with commandos and partisans in World War II, they knew such an organization would be worth its weight in gold. Given the number of potential targets Russia developed through its intelligence services, Spetsnaz came to include over 100,000 men and women, all trained to carry out both overt and covert missions anywhere in the world.

To lead these teams the GRU required only officers who possessed the ultimate ability to lead the caliber of men who wore the wolf's head. Special selection boards were held to discover these young men, whose backgrounds must be fully documented and whose natural skills at dominating their peers and subordinates are unquestioned. Physically they must rank in the upper one percent of their peers. Spetsnaz demanded aggressive, tough people and it got them.

At the close of his four years at Ryazan, Chuikov found himself invited to attend a series of interviews with men he neither knew of nor recognized as being part of the military. Most of the sessions were informal, almost friendly. Upon attending the last meeting he was dismissed. Moments after he'd left the cozy office, Vasili Suworov instructed the school's commander to post young Chuikov to further training as a Spetsnaz candidate.

He'd done well. Soon missions started coming down to the team Chuikov led. At first they were practice in nature, a demolition exercise here, a political kidnapping there. Peter's successes began piling up, and there seemed little the officer and his men couldn't or wouldn't do, no matter the difficulty woven into the play of the problem. Their first live mission came about after Chuikov, now a captain, had been with Spetsnaz for over two years. Ordered into a small country that had been fighting a war of liberation for six long years, Peter's team was instructed to infiltrate one of the enemy government's most secure facilities and assassinate a counterinsurgency expert whose program was beginning to hamper guerrilla activities. Chuikov's deployment was a success, with Peter personally smothering the man in his bed with his own pillow.

Other assassinations followed. Chuikov's star began rising as he and his teams undertook training operations for insurgents in countries so small their names often meant nothing to the world at large. Peter began building training camps for terrorists whose talents the GRU felt were compatible with Soviet total-war doctrine. When the question of how to deal with political dissidents living overseas had to be answered, the GRU sent Chuikov, and soon certain high-profile fist shakers came to enjoy the quiet of the grave or mental hospital. Angola, Chad, Central and South America, they all hosted Chuikov at one time or another. He made rank quickly, earning a reputation for single-minded excellence in Spetsnaz operations. His ability behind a rifle earned him a posting to the Special Warfare Shooting School, where by coincidence Pushkin had met him briefly while the younger officer's team was attending training.

Where and when Colonel Peter Chuikov began to question his role as a Spetsnaz hatchet man, no one could answer except the officer himself. It may have begun with the travel he was allowed because of his job and status. Those in the West obviously lived better and appeared happier than those under the heel of communism. The seed of defection was watered with the flood of blood ordered spilled by men like Suworov, orders carried out time and time again by Chuikov and his agents of fortune. It was one thing to do battle against an enemy trained and armed to resist you, but it was something else again to see whole villages depopulated by chemical warfare and carpet bombings. Although Spetsnaz had hardened Chuikov's mind and body to many things, it had not frozen his soul.

Soon he began planning his escape from the country he'd been born into. There wasn't much he would be leaving behind. His marriage, entered into after he'd been promoted to the rank of major, had fallen apart under the demands of the job he was entrusted with. Lydia became bored with being alone month after month, not knowing where he was or what he was doing away from their tiny apartment. Soon he began hearing stories about her "visitors," often officers and sometimes enlisted men from conventional army units stationed nearby. The GRU had bluntly informed him that his wife had become a barracks slut, sleeping with anyone she fancied and degrading him whenever she could with her lovers. They'd even produced photographs taken in secret. Chuikov's mind had reeled in pain and shock at how his young bride entertained herself while he was living like a dog, maintaining his sanity with thoughts of home and a devoted spouse.

The divorce was arranged by Suworov's legal office, and Lydia was packed up and sent off to a remote city, where she was given a menial job gluing the soles of cheap shoes together before they were shipped as export items to Russia's client states. Peter never asked about her after that, knowing that to do so would diminish him in the eyes of his superiors. The pain of her treachery was soon washed away with the blood he was allowed to let flow in Rhodesia and South Africa, then Central America when that portion of the world began to ripen. Afghanistan was what had finally sickened Chuikov to the point of considering defection. Spetsnaz could not vanquish the sense of decency that still lived deep inside the Soviet officer, but it could help him to survive once he made his move toward the West.

Peter Chuikov, like most other men who joined special-operations units, was basically as much a human being as any of his countrymen. Granted he possessed limits and talents that lent themselves to the kind of work he'd chosen, and in perhaps more bountiful amounts than the average citizen. But Chuikov felt pain, endured grief, struggled against frustration, fear, and failure just as did the postman, milkman, or farmer carving out livings for themselves within the Soviet or any other system of government. He'd found it amusing at first that so many misunderstood his character, thinking him to be some kind of superman or wild animal on a short leash because of his affiliation with Spetsnaz. Later his amusement turned sour as the realization that very few of his fellow Russians understood that whatever peace and security they enjoyed was bought in part by the sacrifices he and his fellow soldiers, sailors, and airmen laid upon the table. Many Spetsnaz commandos had returned to civilian life after their terms of service, only to find that the changes brought about by patriotic duty to the motherland often worked against them in a gentler society, which preferred to pretend the world was a Garden of Eden without serpents in any form.

For this and many other reasons, the Spetsnaz colonel had decided to hang up his weapons and attempt to begin a life he could control. With both parents dead, his ex-wife happily screwing half the factory she worked at, and a legion of dead comrades to keep him company on those lonely nights he was sure to face if he were successful in his escape, Peter Chuikov planned and executed the greatest operation of his career, his own defection.

His eyes popped open with a start as he realized the extent of his fatigue. Somehow Chuikov had allowed himself to drowse, his head bobbing and jerking as his entire life played itself out inside his mind like a documentary. He didn't recognize the man's face just feet from his own, nor did he comprehend his instant reaction to the danger poised by the commando as the man swung the black rifle toward Chuikov's half-hidden form.

In a single motion the colonel raised the short-barreled shotgun from where it lay across his lap, jerking the trigger twice with an equal amount of pumps in between. The Spetsnaz tracker dissolved in a spray of smoke and lead, the buckshot punching a tight pattern into his face and upper chest at the extremely short distance between the two. Peter Chuikov heard the outburst coming from down below as the rest of the dead rifleman's team reacted to the sounds of battle. With a start he grabbed his rucksack with one hand, gripping the shotgun in the other as he began scrambling upward. The Ruger was left where it sat, no time for the Russian to try and strap it to the ruck or sling it over his back. A burst of automatic fire roared over his head, snapping into the trees above him and showering him with bits of wood and leaves. A second rifle joined in, this time the rounds hitting below him as the gunner tried to compensate for the angle of the hill they were on as well as the foliage between him and his fleeing target.

Chuikov's mind registered the sound of an aircraft flying directly overhead. Seconds later he watched as five parachutes blossomed on the horizon less than four klicks away. The Americans had arrived! Digging his feet into the soft earth, the Spetsnaz colonel urged himself to move faster, spinning once to lay down a barrage of shotgun fire, which tore downhill, destroying everything in the path of the whistling pellets. More shouts from his pursuers, and another round of gunfire aimed his way. Chuikov clambered over the hill's crest, the parachutists already on the ground and invisible from where he stood. "LALO," he thought out loud. "Very professional and, considering their situation at the moment, wise as well." Stripping the beacon from its protective container, the Russian flipped two small black switches, then pushed a single red button three times. A green light began to glow from a tiny window in the face of the unit, showing

Chuikov his system was functioning smoothly. Tucking the beacon into the depth of his rucksack, he zipped the bag's top shut and swiftly reloaded the shotgun. Whipping the Beretta out from its holster, the commando emptied all fifteen rounds piecemeal downrange, forcing the sounds of his infuriated followers to cease as they dove into the earth to escape the fusillade. Then Chuikov was running again, running for his life, for his safety, but most of all, for his freedom.

CHAPTER 20

"Everybody's up, Bo! We're ready to move out!" Frank Hartung jerked the charging handle on his Colt Commando, feeling the bolt fly forward as it stripped a round from the magazine he'd loaded before the drop. Hartung's landing had shaken the old master blaster up for a few short seconds, his fall arrested by a half-buried mound of moose bones, the remnants of a wolf pack's feast some years before.

Gunfire from the surrounding hills washed over the team like cold water. "Sounds like our boy's got hisself knee-deep in shit already," commented Silver. "I'll activate our receiver and get a fix on his Russian ass, take just a minute or two."

Thornton nodded. "Might as well be fucking oh nine hundred with all the light we got! I don't know how long this colonel's been in contact, but he's had it tough if they've been chasing him for any length of time."

Bannion agreed. "That's affirmative. Summer up

here's a bitch when it comes to playing hide and seek. They can run him to ground if there's enough of them, or he's wounded. Chuikov must not have thought they'd get onto him as fast as they have. I don't envy his butt right now."

"Got him!" blurted Silver. "Something our colonel doesn't know is that I can literally track him with this unit. One of the shuttles dropped off a gizmo in space last year that we're relaying through right now. NSA programmed our receiver to the frequency he gave Foster. The new dish not only pinpoints the source of the beacon, but it can follow it if the transmitter is moved or being moved."

"So we can lock on to him and you can drive us right to where he is, right?"

"You got it, Bo. That's not gonna be tough, either. From what papa's little black box says, our defector is cutting a husk directly for this DZ."

Bailey, his ass, back, and shoulders still stinging from the triple bounce he'd taken while landing, spoke up. "Listening to the amount of gunfire, I can understand his motivation. We're gonna have to haul ass if he's got even half a chance left. What's the distance, Jason?"

Flipping a switch, the communications expert was rewarded with a digital readout. "A little over four klicks from where we sit. If I recall my map recon correctly, the terrain's not bad. He's coming downhill most of the way, but there's a river that'll cut him off from us. If we can reach that point I can put us across from him where he can see us."

"Let's do it!" ordered Thornton. "We've come too

far to let some buncha Spetsnaz assholes walk away with the brass ring."

As one, the Springbladers leaped to their feet and began jogging after Silver's rapidly moving figure. Ahead they could hear scattered shots as Chuikov's pursuers attempted to close the distance, the boom of a shotgun hanging like a funeral dirge above their heads.

CHAPTER 21

Pushkin shoved his way between the remaining two commandos on his team. At their feet lay Boris's mangled corpse, its features gone. "Damn him to hell!" swore the sweating major. They'd been on Chuikov's trail for hours since Kushkin's beheading; Boris losing, then finding the colonel's ingenious track as he led them across the virgin wilderness toward who knew where. "Two Spetsnaz commandos killed, and we haven't even wounded the bastard! If this keeps up Suworov will be sending teams after us . . . should we survive this madman's skill, that is."

Antonov was busy checking the area where Chuikov had fallen asleep. He and Igor had begun chasing the man as soon as they'd heard the deep boom of the shotgun as it blew bits of Boris all over the woodline. Each commando had expended several magazines in an attempt to bring the fugitive down, only to have to hug the earth themselves as he poured a volley of hand-held cannon fire in their direction. The stinging sound of high-velocity 9-mm rounds had convinced them to pull back until Pushkin could devise their next step, that and the arrival of the American aircraft flying overhead. "He's left his rifle so we no longer need to fear his eye at long range, Comrade Major. I find no blood; it appears the man was resting when our tracker stumbled upon him."

"Why do you say that?" asked Pushkin.

"Chuikov would never let one of us get this close unless he were hurt or asleep. We know he's been on the run for more than ten days already. His resistance is down, his physical being is starting to shut down, especially now that he's outdoors with a minimum of rations available. I believe he simply fell asleep after dragging us all over this cursed land, and Boris failed to get the first shot off."

Igor, quiet until now, finally spoke. He was shocked to the bone that one man had so quickly killed two of his companions, especially since he'd never seen this many Spetsnaz troopers waxed in such a fashion. Even against the *muj* they'd at least have gotten a few solid blows in of their own, but Chuikov was picking them off like flies, and it was supposed to be *them* chasing *him*! "The plane means the Americans are here. What now?"

Pushkin cocked his head to one side, as if he'd forgotten the heavy pulse of the engines overhead as he'd scrambled uphill under the unaimed rounds from Chuikov's weapons. "We push on now! Colonel Chuikov will head directly for the drop zone, we know the plane cannot have landed, so they have jumped people in to fetch their prize. There is no time to wait or plan. Now we can only race against Chuikov's will to win, and our own not to lose.''

Antonov racked a fresh round into his weapon's chamber, a look of determination on his face as he took the point. ''No one goes home, comrades. No one goes home until Chuikov is dead!''

CHAPTER 22

He'd thrown the ruck away after covering half a klick. The weight was draining him of much-needed energy, a thought that shook him as he realized his age for the first time. All he now carried with him was the shotgun, its ammunition, the pistol, and the bowie. The beacon, steadily sending out its message, rode above his heart in one of the full-cut pockets of his Gortex rain jacket. His body was soaked in sweat and he ached to drink from the canteen he'd slung around his neck on a paracord thong. There will be time for water later, he told himself. For now he had to conserve everything from ammunition to the few snack bars he'd stuffed into another pocket in the jacket.

After he'd dropped over the opposite side of the hill he'd lost track of the men chasing him. Chuikov hoped to hell he'd at least winged somebody, considering all the caps he'd busted. In any event, he was once again a hair's breadth ahead of Vasili's war dogs, with two of the foul bastards down and dead. Peter wondered how the Spetsnaz commander was handling two defeats in a row. If he'd been selected by Suworov to lead, then he would be as close to a fury as one could get, thought Chuikov. At the same time the man would really begin to get with the program. He'd have heard the American plane fly overhead and he'd know his time on the ground was limited. Even by chance, if they could catch up with the colonel, there was still the challenge of killing him. After that there was the American team, which Peter plainly hoped wouldn't be a two-man pararescue element with three Marines along. Not that he disliked or thought little of the Marine Corps's ability to perform on the battlefield, it was just that he would hope Foster could scare someone up who understood the threat a Spetsnaz team held. PJs and Marines would be inclined to want to disarm Chuikov before an extraction, and that was not going to happen. Better he lose the Americans and head for Canada than suffer their stupidity while Suworov's angels swarmed around them, eager for the kill.

Taking a second bearing from the compass, Peter began slipping downward toward the river he knew he'd have to cross before having a clear shot at the DZ. Five chutes meant five people. With any luck they were homed in on him now, and as long as he kept moving in a straight line the beacon would be able to perform as intended. As his pickup team had no way of knowing how far away the shooting had taken place from where they had landed, it was imperative that Chuikov gain as much ground as possible. The river would prove difficult, being perhaps impossible to cross where his azimuth

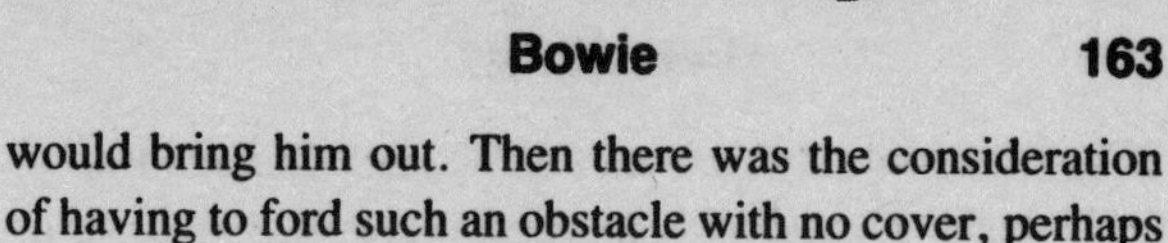

would bring him out. Then there was the consideration of having to ford such an obstacle with no cover, perhaps under the guns of the Spetsnaz team.

Well, shit happens, he told himself. A scurry of movement above him reminded the weary man that the hunt was once again on. Taking a visual bead on a large waterfall off to the left of where his compass was pointing, Chuikov began cascading down the shale-strewn face of the mountain leading to the river's edge. The sounds of his passage drifted upward, reaching the ears of his pursuers and spurring them on as they realized how close they were to their mark.

Antonov saw the bounding figure first, coming to a halt and pressing the stock of his rifle up against a sweat-soaked shoulder. Forcing himself to breathe in shallow gasps, the noncom followed Chuikov's progress, matching his irregular gait with the front sight of the AR-15. A swift squeeze of the trigger was rewarded with the target lurching to a stop, his hand pressed up against the small of his back. Then he was running again. Antonov snapped several more .223 stingers at the man before he floundered into the forest, each one digging up dirt as it impacted a fraction of an inch behind and in front of the wounded man.

"I dusted his hide!" exclaimed Antonov as Pushkin pulled up beside him. "Hit him near the small of the back, missed the spinal cord or he'd be down now. But I've hurt him, that's for certain!"

Ripping huge gouts of oxygen into his lungs through his mouth, Pushkin nodded vigorously. Igor skidded to a stop behind the two men, falling as the loose shale beneath his feet gave way, causing him to lose his balance. "Damn!" grunted the fallen commando as Pushkin helped him to his feet.

"What is down there?" quizzed Pushkin. "Why do I hear that sound, a sound like a hundred cannons going off all at once?"

"It's a waterfall, Comrade Major. We have several near the city I grew up in. This sounds to be a massive piece of work."

Pushkin thanked Igor for his information. You never knew where these men came from, or why they would want to spend their lives the way they'd chosen. Igor was a qualified pilot as well as a commando. In what spare time he had he painted, some of the stuff so good it was hung in Spetsnaz mess halls all over Russia and beyond. What other talents the man possessed, Pushkin wasn't sure; it was a composite team they'd put together.

"We must move now, Major. He may be down, for all I know, or he's going to find somewhere to curl up and wait for the Americans to find him. If he's using a beacon to guide them in it is only a matter of time. We could be facing an entire A-team of Green Berets or a squad of Rangers, should we take too much time."

Pushkin indicated that Antonov should take the lead once again. He hoped his friend would make contact first, killing Chuikov in a face-to-face confrontation. When they got back to Moscow he'd put both men in for decorations, especially Antonov, who deserved the highest award the Kremlin could give for his service to the cause of international communism. The three men began leapfrogging down the hill, small shale slides erupting under their feet as they scooted across the mass

of decaying rock like camouflaged surfers. Each would slide to a stop, covering the other two until it was his turn to begin negotiating the slope's steep angle.

Within minutes they were once again inside the trees, the roar of millions of gallons of water reaching their ears like a giant's brass drum.

Chuikov straightened as the round plowed into his lower left side. He felt the stretching of his stomach muscles as the .223 glanced off a rib, cracking it in two places. The pain caused by his belly blowing open staggered him, only the rock-hard will to survive pushing him into the safety of the trees. Suddenly, through the fog of his wounding, the combat master spotted a well-worn game trail leading downward. Demanding his feet to move toward the tiny highway, Chuikov pulled a dark blue cravat of cotton from the Gortex jacket. Ripping his clothes out from where they were tucked into his waistband, the Spetsnaz officer found the exit hole in his gut by touch, a hunk of off-white gut protruding from the crater like an obscene tongue. His face a coiled mask of unadulterated determination, Chuikov began shoving the cotton plug deep into his gut. The effort dropped him to his knees on the trail, the shotgun falling free as he doubled over in a pain so pure he thought his head would explode. Dark ghostlike creatures swam in front of his eyes. A long chain of bloody drool slipped over his lower lip and sped its way downward, smacking with a puff of dust into the dirt. Chuikov felt his bladder let loose, the warm stream of piss soaking his underwear and gushing down the inside of both his thighs.

"I am badly fucked up," he told himself, the understatement registering even as he said it, bringing a wicked smile to his pale features. Above and behind him he heard the shale as it was displaced by booted feet. Gripping the shotgun in both hands, Peter forced his head, and then his body, up. "I am *Spetsnaz*!" he murmured over and over to himself. "I am Spetsnaz!" The effort nearly killed him right then and there, but all of a sudden he was once again on his feet and staggering down the trail.

Thornton and team were now running for all they were worth. Bo ordered their rucks abandoned after the first hundred meters, leaving them with no more than their LBE and weapons. Silver set a murderous pace, bounding over fallen logs and scampering between rocks that could break a man's ankle in a dozen places if he set a booted foot down wrong. The sound of their breathing was awesome, swallowing them up in a controlled frenzy of locomotion. They were all superbly conditioned, with Hartung at the rear of the column barking encouragement as they raced toward the river. Not one of them would fall out or slow down regardless of whatever physical discouragements their bodies tried to fool them with. Silver kept the receiver gripped tightly in one hand, using the other to balance him as he led his fellow warriors toward their destination, now less than a klick away.

"Human gut." Antonov stood from where he'd knelt briefly, a slimy piece of bloody flesh between his thick fingers. "It's a wonder the man lives after being hit like this," he continued.

Igor nodded, his AR-15 held at the ready, eyes bounc-

ing around in their sockets like two drops of ice-cold water on a hot skillet. "He continues toward the water, like the wounded animal he is. We found his pack but no other guns, so he remains armed . . ."

". . . and therefore dangerous," finished Pushkin. The chase was coming to a close. Pushkin could feel it, could smell it as easily as he smelled the sweet odor of Chuikov's blood on the trail where he'd fallen. The Americans would never reach the Soviet officer in time to help him. Beacons were only good if they were stationary, and Chuikov was anything but that. He could imagine the rescue team's frustration at having to watch their homing device's signals appear and disappear as the wounded man tumbled down the hill. Sooner or later they might stumble onto what Pushkin's men would leave for them to find. It would be a lesson for any future traitors to consider.

"Track him carefully from here on in," advised the triumphant officer. "He still has that damned shotgun of his, and perhaps a pistol and knife. A wounded bear is the worst creature to meet unexpectedly, and that is what our colonel has become."

Pulling Igor back, Antonov strode forward and down the trail. Giving the commando's back a hard slap of encouragement, Pushkin took up the tail gunner's position, sweeping the rear flanks with watchful eyes, looking upward just in case the man had found the strength to climb into a tree to await their arrival. He'd seen wounded men do stranger things in lands much harsher than this. Two dead Spetsnaz veterans testified to Chuikov's adeptness at killing from close range.

Slinking forward for five minutes, they followed the

huge droplets of blood dotting the trail like rose-colored gumdrops. Antonov raised a hand to stop their progress, lying down and sliding out onto a grassy ledge overlooking the river's whitewater rapids below. Scanning the trail as it wound its way down to the water's edge, the noncom was impressed by the sheer beauty of the scene. The waterfall itself rose nearly one hundred feet from the surface of the river it fed. Although only fifty or so feet wide, the sound it made was as deafening as the view was beautiful. Antonov was about to motion the rest of the team forward when a sudden movement caught his eye. Bringing the rifle to bear, he could faintly see Chuikov's figure as the man dragged himself along a rocky ledge leading underneath the protective cover of the fall's hoary white flow. Risking it all, the Spetsnaz marksman emptied a magazine through the misty veil, unsure of his accuracy but convinced of his victim's position. "I have him, Yuri!" the man shouted back to his two companions. "He is beneath the fall itself, on a ledge. I may have hit him, but there's no way to tell except by going in after the bastard."

Tapping Igor on the shoulder, Pushkin gave the man his blessing. Antonov should have waited until they were closer to the colonel before he blasted away. Now, if the man were still alive, he would know how close they were. Pushkin was not concerned in whether or not they'd kill Chuikov, he was concerned with how many of them it would now take to do it. Igor moved forward on cat's feet, the muzzle of his rifle held low in front of him as he tiptoed down the trail in Chuikov's wake. As Pushkin covered the two men from the bluff, he watched with satisfaction as Igor snatched up the abandoned shotgun,

holding it high before tossing it into the river. Fanning out, the two Russians exchanged hand signals as to what they wanted to do. Pushkin would momentarily lose them as the heavy spray coming off the falls would rise up, clouding his bird's-eye view of the action taking place. Anytime now, he told himself. Colonel Peter Chuikov was now history, a legend in his own mind, a score on Pushkin's already impressive record.

CHAPTER 23

The rounds smashed into his lower legs like hornets. Chuikov rolled back against the slick rock wall, feeling fragments of bullet and stone peppering him from all sides. Why he wasn't killed then and there, he didn't know. All that mattered was that he was still alive. Pulling the Beretta from its holster, he watched in dismal fascination as the weapon slipped from his cracked and broken fingers. His attempt to pick it back up failed, the pistol sliding off the ledge and into the bubbling well at its lip. Looking for the knife, he found he'd lost it somewhere back up the trail. Chuikov laid his head back on the coolness of the stone, letting his thoughts fly upward and away from the horror he knew was coming.

It had been a good race. He should have figured Suworov would move faster than one expected of an old man, but that was always the way Vasili worked, fast and in unexpected ways. The gray-haired bastard wouldn't have the satisfaction of seeing the microchips returned though. Chuikov had sent them from Valdez as soon as he'd arrived, to a safe courier in Los Angeles. If Peter didn't make contact in another week the chips would be forwarded to Colonel Foster. That would make both his day and his career, thought Chuikov, smiling. It was the ultimate Spetsnaz move, the best deception being the one you most wanted to believe from the onset.

The Russian felt his legs bleeding badly, not bothering to check them because he knew there was nothing left he could do. Leave it to the Americans to fuck up a rescue operation, he thought gruffly. All their money and the luxury of time had proved only that they remained children at the game of special ops. It seemed to be getting darker inside his frosty cave, then he realized he was beginning to die in earnest. Lydia's face appeared in front of him, her smile warming his belly in remembrance of better times, although few they were. He couldn't hear the waterfall any longer, or he didn't care to. Life had been good, he supposed. It might have been better had he taken more care, moved a bit slower . . . or faster, as it turned out . . . and maybe have approached the British with his deal.

Chuikov felt them coming just as the wolf feels the pack's mood changing when they realize one of their own is down and too weak to fight. Fearing and hating weakness among their own kind more than death itself, they attack, slicing and clawing at their wounded brother until there is nothing left except gristle and bone, the ground beneath a carpet of red. He was that downed wolf, and the pack was nipping at his hindquarters, jerking at his throat, and preparing to remove him from the rolls for all time.

"Fuck 'em," he whispered to the emptiness around him. "I was better than any five of the scum." He closed his eyes to await the reaper's calling with as much dignity as was left him. Outside, the air erupted in gunfire, its sound barely disturbing the sleeping warrior.

CHAPTER 24

Thornton opened up from the far bank, his first burst catching Igor across the chest and dumping him into the whirling river before Antonov could react. The man surfaced for a moment, his hand stretched out to the Russian sergeant in a silent plea for help before the current pulled him back under. Spinning away from the ledge, Antonov raced for the cover of some moss-covered boulders, only to have his legs cut out from beneath him as Hartung smoked a full magazine SEAL style from his hidden position just down from where Thornton had dropped his empty carbine and was now running for the base of the falls.

Pushkin couldn't believe his eyes! Igor's sudden demise seemed at first a joke. How could Chuikov possibly continue to fight? Then the rattle of small-arms fire reached the Soviet major's ears above the din of the falls and he could but watch as Antonov was cut down in midstride. Attempting to lay down a base of fire for his friend and comrade, Pushkin blasted away from his position. For his efforts he was rewarded with a flurry of fire from at least three other weapons he couldn't pinpoint. Drawing back, he realized the mission was a failure. Chuikov could still be alive, and with the Americans in place there was no way he could hope to reverse that fact. Turning to retrace his steps into the forest, Pushkin found himself facing one of God's greatest creatures.

The Alaskan grizzly had been making his way down the trail toward his favorite fishing hole when he noticed the strange smell of man in his domain. Weak of eyesight but powerful of nose, the massive bear had tracked the invader down, and with a huge paw he swept the creature off its feet. Not waiting for the man to rise, the bear rumbled down on top of him, digging his hind feet with their razorlike claws into the soft belly and burrowing both legs downward with all the pressure of the hindquarter's mighty muscles. The scream that came from the furiously fighting figure was lost to those on the other side, who stood watching in mute silence. When the bear was finished, he grabbed hold of a ruptured shoulder, dragging the broken body into the woods, where he could enjoy his meal without being bothered.

Thornton reached the lip of the wide pool and dove in without hesitation. Feeling his way, he kicked upward against the current, coming out just underneath the downpour of water forming the falls' towering face. The figure of a man lay just within his reach. Bo couldn't tell if he was alive or dead. Moving closer, the waterborne warrior pulled the Russian ballistic from its sheath, aiming the deadly blade at the base of the man's throat.

• • •

Chuikov's head rolled to the side. As his eyes opened he saw a face from hell staring at him, the familiar form of a Spetsnaz ballistic knife just inches from his throat. "Ah, you have finally arrived. Kill me and be damned!" With that Chuikov spit directly into Thornton's face.

"Motherfucker!" spit Thornton back. Easing off the knife's trigger, he sheathed it. Then, pulling the man along the ledge as he fought the steady current with one hand, Bo finally reached the end of the stone platform, where Mike was waiting to take over. Once up on dry land they could hear the Blackhawk coming in, its medical crew alerted through Silver's quick thinking in bringing along a pocket-sized radio for FM communications in case they needed help.

"He gonna live?" asked Frank.

"Who knows? If he doesn't, at least we gave it our best shot. Where's the boys from Spetsnaz?"

Turning away to watch Bailey guide the National Guard bird in, Hartung pointed vaguely across the river. "Two dead from gunshots, the third met some big hairy fella who invited him to lunch. I don't think we need concern ourselves with him, though."

Thornton gazed across to where Hartung was pointing, only seeing the beauty of the Alaskan wilderness. Next to him, Chuikov squeezed Bo's hand in a message both men understood.

Colonel Peter Chuikov was finally a free man.

CHAPTER 25

Bannion assumed the classic pathfinder's pose, both arms outstretched so that from behind he looked like a huge T. The chopper settled into its glide pattern, a pararescueman standing tall on either skid, their medical kits slung over their backs as they prepared to touch down and assist Thornton's team with the firefight's casualties. Off to one side of the hasty LZ knelt Silver, the handheld FM radio pressed against his rapidly moving lips as he talked the pilot down. A second bird maintained an orbit several klicks out, waiting to pick up whoever was left on the deck once the medivac pulled pitch for Fort Richardson in Fairbanks.

Thornton was busily hitting the injured Russian colonel's wounds with everything he had. Double Ace-Wraps around the legs to quench the flow of blood, an IV quickly punched into place to replenish the man's lost body fluids, a syrette of morphine to smother the pain Chuikov was obviously in, everything administered swiftly and efficiently as Bo relied on years of experience and training to accomplish his tasks.

"He looks a little better, if looking like shit is better than how we found him, that is."

Thornton nodded at Hartung's observation. "Poor bastard musta thought I was one of his own. Rapped off a line of Russian when I grabbed hold of him, then spit in my face."

Hartung laughed, the sound buried by the wall of turbine-induced noise from the airframe perched atop Mike's hastily chosen LZ. Yelling to make himself heard, the veteran told his team leader he thought he'd pull a short recon of the opposite bank, just in case one of the Spetsnaz killers might be alive. Thornton agreed, backing off from Chuikov as the PJs ran up, telling him with a series of nods and hand signals they would now be taking over. As the best trauma specialists in the business did a rapid evaluation of Thornton's handiwork, the two Springbladers dropped back toward the falls.

"We'll leave Mike and the ranger here to cover our asses. I want Bailey going out with Chuikov as an escort all the way back to friendly hands. The devil only knows who will be waiting for the 'Hawk to land, and I sure as hell don't want the Company or FBI slipping our boy out from under our noses after all we've been through."

Hartung grunted in agreement. Turning so that he had eye contact with the rest of the team, Hartung relayed a burst of hand-and-arm signals to each man, indicating where he should go and what both the sergeant major and Thornton were planning. Bailey was the first to acknowledge his new set of instructions, loping up behind the PJs and scrambling aboard the Blackhawk as the massive airship began to lift off. Bannion and Silver, who'd been providing a protective overwatch during the evac sequence, leapfrogged down to the river's edge, where they took up positions from which they could cover Thornton and Frank while they reconned the other side. Everyone ducked as the NG helo's pilot kicked the afterburners in, the powerful chopper twisting in midair and climbing rapidly for the safety of the skies. Thornton returned Bailey's wave with a thumbs-up of his own, and suddenly it was quiet except for the roar of the falls and the rush of the water heading downriver.

Silver signaled that he'd instructed their pickup ship to stand off for several more minutes, receiving a curt nod from Thornton, who was entering the cold torrent from which he'd already made a round trip. Bannion and Silver began sweeping the opposite bank with their Colts, ready to frag any sign of opposition that might raise its ugly head once the recon team was vulnerable. Hartung slipped into the heady undertow behind Bo, his rifle slung as each man needed both hands free to pull himself along the rock outcropping that stretched from one side of the waterway to the other. It only took them a couple of minutes to complete their fording, tension high, as no one knew for sure if the Spetsnaz team was out of action or simply playing possum. Slipping onto the shoreline like a snake, Thornton rapidly crawled into the knee-high tender grasses, which barely hid his combat-ready figure from the cover team. Hartung was next, choosing to scamper past Bo and over to a pile of moss-covered boulders from which he could cover the One-Zero as he moved deeper into the tree line.

Thornton threw a glance toward Bannion, who gave

the big commando a high-five, indicating everything looked good from where the two riflemen lay. Confirming his unspoken intentions with Frank, Bo began making his way toward the spot where Pushkin had encountered Mr. Bear, the sounds of bones breaking and liquids spilling reaching his ears as he moved into the shadow of the forest. Inside Bo knew it was all over. He'd seen the one Russian soldier disappear under the pounding of the torrent that had swept him away once the team's guns had blown him off the shore. Hartung had reported the other Soviet dead, although Bo wasn't sure where or how that had taken place. He'd have to leave it to Frank, who was even now pulling drag behind him as he inched his way up the steep bluff toward the bear buffet taking place above him. A rapid scramble brought Thornton to the place where Pushkin had met his fate, a swatch of bloody ground and torn uniform bits marking the spot. Unhooking a grenade just in case the grizzly wasn't full, Thornton pushed his way toward the picnic now fully under way. Looking down, he spotted a document pouch ripped from its perch on Pushkin's combat harness, the carrier sticky with human blood but undamaged.

Seconds later Thornton's mind reeled as he watched the massive creature sink its long blunt nose deep inside Pushkin's ravaged carcass, teeth and tongue working in unison like a monstrous weed eater as the beast swallowed a double handful of human entrails. Bo began gagging slightly, the smell of the bear and its feed combining so that the odor was overpowering in the sweet mist of the falls' spray. Checking his natural reaction to the primitive scene being played out before him, the Springblader squatted, forcing himself to witness the end of Major Yuri Pushkin at the paws of the man's own national symbol. Ironic, Bo thought to himself as the grizzly found the exploded heart muscle with an inquisitive paw, the Russian bear devours its own much the same. The Soviet Union was actually nothing more than a band of captive satellite nations, held in check by the might and hunger of Russia itself. Thornton recoiled in horror as the immense bear lifted its great shaggy head skyward, issuing a contented belch, which began deep within its now-full belly.

Slowly the former Green Beret turned on his heels, slinking quietly away from the fleshy orgy now burnt forever into his mind's eye. It was time to go home.

Frank was like a huge camouflaged cat. Bent low over the black carbine, his head upright so that his piercing eyes could sweep back and forth, up and down, without constraint, he shuffled forward toward the spot where the Russian had dropped from sight. Hartung knew he'd hit the big Soviet hard with a sustained burst of .223 tendonizers, which had spun the Spetsnaz commando around like a top as they ripped through his legs. There was a chance some of the bullets had torn into the soldier's lower abdomen, in which case the man should be stone cold dead somewhere near where Hartung was creeping. Frank knew, however, that the dead didn't necessarily stay that way, having watched more than one man in his long career as a professional warrior come back from massive wounds to pull the trigger just one more time before catching the boat to the other side.

Hartung heard the familiar rasp of the ballistic as it left its steel housing. Half turning, he knew he would be too late to avoid the deadly sting of the Russian spring-blade, fired from ambush not more than ten feet away. Frank felt the spring-propelled blade graze his cheek, its razorlike tip neatly slicing it open so that a veil of blood cascaded down his face in a torrent of crimson. Dropping to one knee, the Sogger was already squeezing his Colt's trigger when he realized the man he was facing was near death anyhow. Antonov's sallow face stared out from beneath a thick roof of berry bush, where the mortally wounded man had dragged his broken body after Hartung's burst collided fatally with his legs.

"As you Americans say," rasped the dying man, "close but no cigar."

Hartung warily watched as the empty launcher rolled out of the Russian's hand. "How bad you hit?" he asked, knowing it was both one of the dumbest yet most important questions any soldier could ask another.

"It is very bad," wheezed Antonov. "You needn't worry about dying, American. There is no gain in your death now."

Hartung glided up to within an arm's reach of the ruined noncom. Carefully lowering himself to the soft ground, Frank sat Indian style in front of the man, the Colt across his upper thighs, the barrel inches away from the terminally wounded soldier's head. "It was me who shot you, thought you'd want to know for some reason."

Antonov laughed weakly, then stared hard at the man who had taken his life. There was a recognition between the two combat soldiers, a recognition untouched by their differing political ideals and morals. They were warhorses, tried by battle and bred by the best in their business. "Your name?" asked Antonov.

"Hartung. Frank Hartung, retired."

Antonov burped a bright wad of blood from between his lips, the sight of it causing Hartung to turn away for a moment in embarrassment. "You are the same Frank Hartung who was in Vietnam? Korea, too, I believe. Yes?"

Hartung returned the man's questioning gaze. "Yeah. How'd you recognize the name?"

A squeak of laughter dribbled out of Antonov's mouth as he enjoyed the moment of confusion on Hartung's face. "We are much the same, my friend," he replied. "Spetsnaz has its files, and we have our area studies much as your own Special Forces does. You are somewhat of a legend to us, although I thought you'd retired from this business last year."

It was Frank's turn to laugh. "Well, I had, Ivan. But this shit gets in your blood. . . ."

A long fit of coughing and near-choking racked Antonov's body as Hartung spoke. For a moment it looked as if the man would die, but the Russian noncom drew deeply from the well of his iron-hard gut, and soon he was quiet again. "How's the pain? You want something for it?"

A grateful look broke through the encrusted sweat and dirt on the Russian's face. "No. I have fought with and against pain all my life, Frank. It is bad, no? But not so bad that I can't conquer it until death's door opens for me. The others, my comrades, they are all dead?"

"Yeah, we nailed 'em all except for one a fucking bear chewed up. Three all together with you . . . that was your team size, wasn't it?"

Antonov nodded, any attempt at duplicity gone as he

felt yet another knot unravel in his fight to stay alive. "The one on the bluff was our commanding officer, Major Pushkin. A bear, you say? How fitting an ending for a Spetsnaz officer, wouldn't you agree, Frank?"

"Fuck if I know. Looked to me like the bear beat the living shit outta this Pushkin bastard. My partner's checking on the remains right now."

"Chuikov?"

Frank sighed at the question, knowing his answer would break the professional soldier's heart. "He's alive. You nearly succeeded but we got to him in time. I think he'll make it."

Antonov couldn't hold the pain back any longer. His body arched itself backward, the pool of blood underneath him widening despite his attempts to staunch it, using strips torn from his battle tunic after he'd been hit. Hartung watched the man's eyes bulge as he fought against the urge to cry out, saw the tip of the tongue severed as bone white teeth bit through tender pink flesh. Stripping a morphine syrette from his shoulder harness, Frank swore at all the men who sent others into battle, knowing this Russian and he were brothers in some crazy way.

Pushing the rifle away so that he could kneel over Antonov, Frank jammed the needle its full length into the man's meaty shoulder. Squeezing the full load into the Soviet, he watched as the morphine took effect, calming and smoothing the way for the man to die in some form of peace. "Thank you, Frank." The whisper was so low Hartung could barely hear the words as they tumbled lazily out of the Russian's mouth. Carefully so as not to alert the almost sleeping man, Frank pulled a second syrette from its pouch, quickly pushing it through Antonov's camouflage uniform so that the needle sank deeply into the man's other arm. "Sleep well, Sarge. You've served your time and done your job, no need dying like a dog when you've a friend close by to guide you across."

Frank Hartung sat quietly as the Russian's breathing slowed to nothing. Patting the now-peaceful soldier on the shoulder, he removed both syrettes, slipping them into one of his ammo pouches. Closing his eyes for a moment, Hartung offered a brief prayer for the warrior beside him, then, hearing Thornton's approach, he pulled the dead Russian out from his thorny lair and signaled Bannion and Silver that all was well.

CHAPTER 26

Linda could hear the two men laughing through the half-open sliding glass door that separated the outdoor deck from the expansive living room. She couldn't help smiling to herself as she moved about the kitchen preparing a pot of strong black coffee for after dinner. It had been a wonderful evening, with Frank, Jason, Calvin, and Mike leaving a half hour earlier for some late-night rambling in the clubs and bars of Seaside, just up the coast. The Russian colonel was a charmer, even though he was still confined to a wheelchair despite two months of rehabilitation at Walter Reed. She found him attractive as well as intelligent, a combination of traits seldom found in men, she reminded herself. Calvin had contacted Bo several weeks earlier, passing on the colonel's desire to meet with the team as a whole. It was Thornton's brainstorm to bring everyone together at his Cannon Beach retreat, with Chuikov getting the doctor's blessing to spend a few extra days on the coast recuperating. Bailey would be his watchdog, the narc needing some R and R himself, given the pace Springblade was operating at.

Noticing she'd left her Glock 19 near the swinging door between the kitchen and living room, Linda deftly scooped it up and slipped the lightweight automatic into the small of her back. Bo had demanded she learn how to shoot, getting her the Glock after his return from Alaska. She'd been surprised at how easy the weapon was to handle, and Thornton had been delighted at her rapid progress on the combat pistol range he'd constructed on their property. Linda was a natural shot, comfortable with a handgun and damned accurate, too. If her mother *ever* found out the young woman was slowly being groomed to take part in the quieter end of the team's missions, she'd probably ask to be put away. Linda's parents were good people, just horribly liberal, which translated as ignorant to Bo's way of thinking.

Pouring the steaming coffee into deep mugs bought by Bo in San Francisco during an earlier contract, Linda considered what she'd learned since Chuikov's arrival at their home. The Spetsnaz colonel's intelligence, brought out in the form of computer microchips, had shaken the Russian threat against Alaska to its very core. Scores of arms caches were uncovered, agents arrested, communication networks disrupted, and political questions answered. It had been a tremendously successful operation for all those concerned, but especially for Chuikov, who'd nearly died in his attempt for freedom. Linda was stunned by the revelations the Russian shared with her as they visited, about events and activities all over the world that she had thought the media knew the truth of. Assassinations that looked like accidents, disasters brought about by carefully laid plans and betrayals, reputations ruined and established through the meticulous planning of the GRU, and carried out by Spetsnaz teams from both the army and navy. She was privy to a world unknown or unsuspected by her friends and peers, and it made her both sorrowful and powerful at the same time.

Dismissing her somber thoughts, the beautiful girl who shared Bo Thornton's life slipped back out onto the cedar decking the two of them had laid, placing the captains mugs between the two men as they acknowledged her with casual nods and heartfelt smiles. Bo reached out to slap the girl's buttocks lightly, murmuring a quiet "Thank you," which was echoed by Chuikov in his native Russian. Seeing the two men were wrapped in conversation, meaning "man talk," she kissed them on the forehead and slid the heavy glass door shut behind her as she returned to the security of the house.

Outside she could hear the heavy pounding of the surf far below the cliff's lip, a three-quarter moon pouring soft yellow light through the three skylights built into the high-beamed ceiling above her. She knew Bo wouldn't be to bed until much later, and only then after he'd helped Chuikov into his own. The two were like brothers, it seemed, a relationship blossoming between the two warriors ever since Bo had pulled the near fatally wounded Russian out from beneath a watery tomb several months before. Linda recalled Calvin's hint that Chuikov might join the Springblade team once his debriefings were completed and a lengthy background investigation finished, something Bo hadn't objected to.

Popping the Glock from its enviable position, the girl tossed it onto the massive bed she and the Springblade One-Zero shared. Within minutes she was nude and under the heavy comforter given them as a housewarming present by Frank. The ocean's steady beat, like that of a massive heart, lulled her into a deep sleep, the Glock and all it stood for forgotten as the antique grandfather clock in Bo's den chimed midnight.

"You are a lucky man, Bo. I have often dreamed of having a place such as yours where I can sit in peace, forgotten by my world and a part of everyone else's." Peter Chuikov, former Spetsnaz colonel, sat comfortably in his wheelchair rubbing the calves of his legs, which were healing nicely. In his lap lay Bo's Browning Hi-Power, its magazine loaded to capacity. He was facing the ocean, listening to his newfound friend's stories of wars and friends past, content that his decision to leave Russia had been both wise and timely. Reports from the NSA and CIA confirmed a major shake-up in the GRU, with new blood coming to power. The emergency sessions held in Moscow because of the Spetsnaz failure to kill Chuikov had been particularly nasty, with an entire chain of command relieved for incompetence in the matter. The American government was extremely happy with how the turn of events were affecting Soviet interests worldwide, using Chuikov's insider information on other GRU operations to dismantle and disrupt Russia's hidden agendas the world over.

"Yeah, it's been a long time coming, Peter. Linda

kinda came along with the package and you can give her all the credit when it comes to our place here. The girl's poured her heart into the house, plus doing her own thing in town and helping Jason get a business of his own started.'' Thornton reached around to grab a thick cigar from the box sent out by Conrad Billings with Calvin. Snipping its ends, he lit up, blowing the smooth smoke over the balcony, where it was swept away in the gentle breeze coming off the sea.

Chuikov sipped at his coffee, both men quiet as each drank in the tranquility of the moment they shared. Once enemies because of their political beliefs, the two had found a common bond in their chosen profession. Peter had fought in many of the same places as Thornton, carrying out daring and often unmentioned operations against whoever the Kremlin sent him against. Bo was stunned at the man's history, learning for the first time that Chuikov had been searching for him while Thornton was detached to Afghanistan, his orders from the GRU to capture or kill the American adviser whose efforts were guiding the freedom fighters in their quest to displace the Russian bear from his foothold in their country. Bo found himself enjoying the man's company and secretly hoping he'd be interested in serving in at least an advisory spot with Springblade once he was cleared.

''Your CIA and NSA both want me to work for them once I've healed. What do you think of their offer, Bo? Would I be comfortable with them or are they just mirrors of our own security services in Russia?''

Thornton flicked a heavy ash from the end of his cigar. Remembering Lippman and all the other professional ''diplomats'' and paper tigers throughout his career, he knew exactly what State and its intelligence puppets had in mind for the colonel. "They'll want you around until, like a flashlight battery, you're used up and no good anymore. Then they'll find some other poor slob and squeeze all they can from his nuts. There's no percentage in playing their game, Peter. You and I are soldiers, not politicos. We've never understood how the other side plays the game and we never will.

"Myself? Well, the boys and I have been fortunate enough to be offered a game whose rules we understand and can play by. Shit, Frank and I have enough going with our Heavy Hook projects to keep us flush in cash for the rest of our lives. Calvin and Mike'll do well with the DEA, especially with the war in Colombia scheduled to last at least a decade. And Jason is sure to hit it off with the artsy-fartsy crowd once Linda gets him on his feet with this new gallery she's put together up in Seaside. We're not stupid. There'll be a time when one of us will want to drop out of the guns-and-guts game and just relax. But to do that we need a civilian occupation to keep us in the manner we've become accustomed to, and deserve.

"You go to work for the feds and you'll end up with shit. Maybe a gold-plated Timex and a retirement, which might pay the rent and for enough newspaper subscriptions so you can keep up with the 'help wanted' ads, but that's about it."

"So maybe I should go to work for you, Bo? Billings tells me your team is President Bush's secret weapon these days. Bailey let it slip you've handled four missions or—how do you businessmen say—'contracts' ever since being activated. Soon I will be well enough to get around on my own, and those who pester me with questions about Iran and Nicaragua will lose interest when they see I'm not looking for a GS-15 rating. Is there something for a former Spetsnaz soldier with Springblade?''

Thornton fixed the smiling man with an amused look of cool appraisal. ''For a price?''

Chuikov laughed loudly, the sound mixing with Thornton's cigar smoke and the ocean's breeze as easily as water does with good scotch. ''Of course for a price, my friend! I am an American soon. There will be bills to pay, credit cards to apply for, debts to incur, and things to buy and invest in if I am to become a good capitalist.

''Naturally I will want only what you feel I am worth, and in whatever currency our Uncle Sam prefers to pay me in.''

Both men laughed. Thornton lay his cigar down and drank deeply from the still-hot mug. ''We could use you, Peter. There's always a place for a man with the kind of experience you have, and our contracts are getting tougher, as Bush relies on us more and more. Your knowledge and insight would give us an advantage we don't have right now. Springblade could go international with you on our team, something I think Billings is getting probed about even now.

''Once you've healed up and shaken the goons loose, we'll talk. Until then you're a welcome guest here. Our home is yours for as long as you like or need.''

Chuikov nodded his head in appreciation. Over the last few months he'd become aware of his isolation; he was a man alone in a strange country that still didn't trust or accept him. There were no longer ties in Russia, his family gone long ago. He would be hated by his former comrades, a constant reminder to them of a betrayal so loathesome they would be eager to avenge themselves if the chance ever came to pass. In Thornton, Hartung, Silver, Bannion, and Bailey he'd found a home where he was accepted as just what he was and wished to become. If Peter Chuikov had a future, it would begin with Springblade, and in fact, it already had.

"Time for me to turn in, comrade. You want some help getting to bed?"

"No, that isn't necessary, Bo. And you can drop the 'comrade' shit. I'm just another bum down on his luck, like the rest of you malcontents. It is a lovely evening and I think I would like to smoke one of your fine cigars and perhaps drink a snifter of brandy, if you've some close by. I'll make my own way to bed, Linda kindly pulled the covers down while I was talking to her about the state of journalistic freedom in Mother Russia."

"Oh," said Bo as he prepared to recover a bottle of very good brandy from the bar in the living room. "I didn't know Russia had any journalistic freedoms. . . ."

"They don't," replied Chuikov dryly. "Our First as well as Second Amendments come from the barrel of a gun . . . which is pointed *at* rather than *by* the people."

"I'll get that brandy and then wish you good night, Colonel." With hardly a sound Bo padded into the living room, where his well-stocked bar stood waiting. Returning to the deck several minutes later, he slid the door wide open, setting the dusty bottle down and picking up a beautifully knit blanket which he snugged around the soundly sleeping Russian's chest and shoulders.

Above them the sky filled with stars as the coast lost the last of its protective cloud cover. For a time Springblade was at ease, and Bo Thornton was at peace with himself in the company of new friends and old soldiers.